SHIRLEY HILT

Silent Screams

This is a work of fiction. The events and characters described herein are imaginary and are not intended to refer to specific places or living persons. The opinions expressed in this manuscript are solely the opinions of the author and do not represent the opinions or thoughts of the publisher. The author has represented and warranted full ownership and/or legal right to publish all the materials in this book.

Silent Screams

v3.0

Outskirts Press, Inc.
http://www.outskirtspress.com

ISBN: 978-1-4327-2756-7

Library of Congress Control Number: 2012913651

PRINTED IN THE UNITED STATES OF AMERICA

Silent Screams

Nana and Gramps walked up the church steps, each clutching one of my hands, and giving me a swing at the top. Once inside, Nana stopped to exchange pleasantries with neighbors, and then we took our seats in the middle pew to the left. Unlike most children my age, I didn't fidget or get bored when the sermon started. I listened intently, trying hard to understand the message the minister was sharing with us.

After the service, Nana and Gramps stopped to shake hands with Pastor Thomas and tell him how much they enjoyed the sermon. The Pastor knelt down to tell me how proud he was that I was so attentive, and such a good little girl. Then he turned to Nana and said, "I have never seen a three year old behave so perfectly. I'm very impressed!"

The Pastor had no way of knowing how much that little country church, or the messages of love, forgiveness, and salvation meant to me. I felt a unique closeness to God that few children my age would ever understand. I looked forward to Sundays, and the Peace that I would feel on that day and that peace would have to carry me through the hell of the days that would follow.

Our lives on the little dirt farm that Nana and Gramps owned was not easy. They barely eked out a living, but we always had food on the table, and a roof over our heads, although it was badly in need of repair. The house was old and small, and the furnishings were tattered, but clean. There were two bedrooms, but my mother, Judy, had one of them, and I had a small cot in the corner of Nana and Gramps' room. What few clothes I had took up one off Nana's dresser drawers, and my two Church dresses hung on hangers in her closet.

One would think that I would share the bedroom Judy had, especially since she was hardly there, but I preferred the arrangement as it was. Judy was sixteen years old, with the body of a grown woman, and the temperament of a wildcat. It was hard to imagine that a person so mean and cantankerous could be the off spring of Nana—who was a loving, God fearing woman. Gramps was Judy's step-father, but had been in her life since she was my age. When I would ask Nana why Judy was so mean, Nana would simply say that Judy was the cross she had to bear. I didn't really understood what she meant by that, but pretended to.

Judy hadn't been home for a few days, and I was ashamed to admit that I was glad. Life was so simple and peaceful when she was gone. Nana and I would help Gramps with the chores, and we would play hide and seek, and other silly games and Nana would always tell me Bible stories before I went to sleep. Life was not luxurious or frivolous, but it was good.

When Gramps old pickup truck rattled into the drive at home, I was disappointed to see a car parked there. That could only mean one thing—Judy was back. My heart sank, and I snuggled a little closer to Nana, hoping that this would be one time I wouldn't regret seeing my mother. I may have been only three years old, but I knew she hated me, and I was terrified of her.

Judy came bounding out of the house, the screen door slamming behind her. She clutched the hand of a handsome young man in uniform, and stopped at the truck to introduce us to him. His name was Robert, and he was a private in the Army, stationed at the base outside of the big city about 200 miles from our little town. When Nana asked if he knew how old Judy was, Judy shot Nana a look that even I understood. John answered, "I know she's only sixteen, but when she turns eighteen, I intend to make her my wife."

We got out of the truck, and Robert knelt by me. "This must be your little girl." He said to Judy. "She is a little doll. What's your name, honey, and how old are you?"

"Lizbeth," I shyly replied, holding up tree fingers. He picked me up and swung me around. " I brought a present for you." He carried me over to the car, reached inside and brought out a brightly wrapped package. Then he placed me on the ground and handed me the package. I held it gingerly, not sure what to do. "Go ahead—open it," Robert told me. "I hope you like it."

I looked to Judy, not wanting to get on her wrong side this early in the visit. She rolled her eyes and said, "Well, go on—open it!" I tore the paper away and took the lid off the box, and nestled inside was a beautiful baby doll, all dressed in pink lace. I could feel my eyes light up when I saw her—I had never owned anything so beautiful!

We all went in the house, and while Nana and Judy made dinner, I sat on Robert's lap, and he told me what life would be like after he married my mother. He said he loved children, and I would want for nothing. I would glance at Judy once in awhile, shocked because she was helping Nana—which she never did, and was actually smiling and being pleasant. It was a side of her I rarely saw, and was a little apprehensive, waiting for the real Judy to show her ugly head. But, she never did, and it was a pleasant afternoon.

When it came time for Robert to leave, he told Nana and Gramps what a pleasant time he had, how much he enjoyed the meal, and that he looked forward to seeing them again. He explained that he would be leaving on 'maneuvers' in a week or so, but hoped he could stop by when he got back. He knelt down in front of me to say goodbye, and gave me a big hug. Then he got into his car and drove off. I hugged my doll tightly, feeling sad because I had a feeling I would never see him again.

After he left, I changed into my everyday dress and readied myself to help Gramps with the evening chores. I was surprised when Judy offered to help too. She hated the farm and anything to do with it and had never helped with feeding the animals. "I don't care if they all starve'" she would proclaim if her helping was suggested by Nana.

In all the excitement, I had forgotten about Freckles. I mentioned this fact to Gramps, and he declared, "Freckles shall be served first!" And we both let out a chuckle.

"Who the hell is Freckles?" Judy asked. I hurriedly explained that Freckles was the spotted pony Gramps had brought home the week before. Granted, he was one step away from the glue factory, and that's probably the only way Gramps could afford him, but he was mine, and I loved him unconditionally.

"What a god-awful ugly animal," Judy said, screwing up her face in distain. "How anyone can love something this ugly is beyond me. But, Nana and Gramps love you—and look at how ugly you are!"

I had my arms flung around Freckles neck, and immediately became self conscious of my long, gangly legs and knobby knees. I knew all my ugly features—Judy had pointed them out to me often enough. My ears stuck out, and I had a long, skinny neck with a "pin" head on the end of it. Freckles nuzzled my neck as if to say he loved me, no matter how ugly I was.

Gramps asked, "How about you ride Freckles around while I do chores?" He knew that would erase from my mind the cutting barb Judy had sent my way. I danced around with anticipation as Gramps put the halter on Freckles. Then he lifted me on the pony's back, and I was in another world. We wondered all around the barnyard, following Gramps as he did the chores. Judy had soon bored of the farm routine and had long ago gone back to the house. When the chores were done, we took Freckles back to the barn and bedded him down for the night, but not before I gave him a big hug and kiss goodnight.

I got ready for bed and hugging my new doll tightly, snuggled down in my cot, while Nana tucked me in and prepared to tell me a Bible story. Gramps and Judy started arguing in the kitchen, and Nana whispered, "It's not a good time—I'll tell you two tomorrow night." Then she hurried out of the room.

"What in the Sam-hill is the ruckus about in here?" Nana asked as she entered the room.

"I was just trying to tell her to watch what she says to Lizbeth. She was out there telling her she was ugly. She's a beautiful child, and she should be proud of her!" I couldn't help but love Gramps as he said that. I decided to close my ears to the loud voices and count the things I loved, and that loved me. Let's see, there's Nana and Gramps, and Freckles, and my dolly, and the Pastor at church, and God and........

The next morning I awoke to the smell of frying bacon. I jumped from the bed, into my clothes and ran into the kitchen to tell Nana what a beautiful day it was going to be. I stopped dead in my tracks when I saw Judy glaring over a hot cup of coffee. Nana gave me a hug and a kiss and asked if I was hungry. She sat me at the table and presented a plate with an egg, some bacon and a biscuit on it. Everything was from our farm, and the biscuit was made by Nana's own hand. Even the honey I drizzled over the biscuit had come from Gramps' "secret bee hive."

Judy finished her coffee, and when Nana asked if she would like some breakfast, she almost shouted, "If I wanted anything to eat—it certainly wouldn't be that slop," slammed her coffee cup down, and stomped off to her bedroom.

I cleaned my plate, and even requested another biscuit, all the while proclaiming how good everything was, trying to reassure Nana that I didn't think it was slop. She patted my arm and gave me her "it's all right, baby" smile, and I scampered off to find Gramps.

Gramps was in the barn. It reeked of old hay, older, rotting wood, and animals. One of the cows was having trouble having a calf, and Gramps was trying to help her. Gramps had beads of sweat across his face, a worried look in his eyes, and breathlessly told me, "Quick, go get Nana!" I ran back to the house as fast as I could, screaming "Nana! Nana!"

Nana and Judy both collided with me at the screen door. "What's wrong, child?" Nana asked. All I could get out was "Gramps" and they both started running for the barn, with me trailing after them as fast as I could go.

When we got to Gramps, he was holding a newborn calf, and trying to blow air in its mouth. Nana explained that the calf wasn't breathing, and that Gramps was trying to get its lungs started. Gramps finally gave up, wiped his brow, and declared," What a shame, such a fine looking calf." Then he looked at me and said, "I guess God needed a little calf in heaven." I knew then that the calf was going to a better place.

I ran over to give Gramps a hug—bloody hands and all. Without thinking, he hugged me back, getting blood on my arms and dress. Judy, who had been standing quietly in the shadows said, "Come on Lizbeth, let's go do some of the chores while Gramps cleans this up." I was taken completely by surprise, and looked at Nana questioningly. She also looked surprised, but smiled and nodded. I walked out of the barn with Judy.

Judy walked to the porch on the side of the house, and picked up the bucket of slop. "Guess we might as well get that hog fed," she said as she motioned towards the pig pen. The hog had a new litter of piglets, and I was telling Judy how tiny and cute they were. When we got to the pen, the hog came running, eagerly awaiting her bucket of scraps. Judy started to empty the bucket, and then stopped midair. "I have an idea! While the momma's here eating, you can go to the other side, climb in and hold one of the babies!"

I tried to tell her that Gramps never let me near the babies, but Judy insisted, saying, "That's because they were too little. They're bigger now, so you won't hurt them. Go ahead, it's ok."

Her explanation made sense to me, and I was secretly dying to hold one of the piglets, so I quickly ran around and climbed in the pen. The piglet that I tried to pick up started squealing as loud and frantically as it could. I looked over my shoulder and saw the huge sow headed straight for me, and she did not have the look of love in her eyes.

I dropped the piglet and turned to run, but my feet were slipping in the mud. The sow hit me full force in the middle of my back, and I went sprawling head first into the mud. The sow turned to check on her litter, and I think to gather more speed, and headed for me again. By this time I had managed to get to my knees, but the sow hit me again, taking a big chunk out of my arm. I was screaming for someone to help me, but Judy was standing by the fence, laughing so hard that she was doubled over. The hog plowed me one more time, again nipping my arm, and was getting ready to charge again, when Gramps lifted me up from the mud hole.

Blood was streaming from my arms, and the sow made a charge towards Gramps. Before I knew it, Nana was at his side, and let the sow have a hardy crack on its snout with a board she had in her hands. Gramps lifted me over the fence, then he was over it, grabbed me up in his arms and heading for the house, Nana hot on our trail.

I was trembling with fear, and crying in pain. My arms were gushing blood from two gaping wounds. Nana grabbed two cloths, and while she applied pressure to one, Gramps applied pressure to the other gash. "I think they need stitches," Nana gasped. "Can you hold both cloths while I get the truck?" Gramps asked Nana. She nodded yes as he headed for the door.

In a flash, the old truck was grumbling by the screen door. Gramps opened the passenger door while he held me as Nana climbed in. He carefully placed me on her lap. As he was running to the driver's side, Judy came running out, a bag in tow, and climbed in the back.

The next thing I knew we were at Doc Taylor's house, and I was lying on a big table in his office. Gramps was talking to me the whole time the doctor was stitching up my arm. He was trying to make me laugh by saying how we would all have to take a bath when we got home—and it wasn't even Saturday night. Then he wrinkled his nose and said, "You remind me of one of those little piglets—cute as the dickens, but you stink to high heaven!" I was forced to let go of a giggle with that one.

Gramps thanked the doctor, and told him he'd settle up when he brought me back to get the stitches out. He carried me out to the truck, where Nana and Judy was waiting. Judy was leaning against the side of the truck, smoking a cigarette and as soon as I was safely on Nana's lap, Gramps turned to Judy and asked her, "What the hell where you doing, letting her get in that pen with that sow?!? I thought you would have better sense than that!!"

"I was feeding the hog, and next thing I knew, Lizbeth was in the pen with one of the piglets. What was I suppose to do?" Judy lied to Gramps, and gave me a look that let me know there would be serious repercussions if I said anything differently. Gramps looked questioningly at me, and I said, "It's my fault, Gramps." I hated myself for lying to him, but even at my tender age, I had honed in on some survival skills.

"Why don't you drop me by the bus station, and I'll get out of your hair for awhile," Judy suggested. I looked hopefully at Gramps, and he nodded and motioned Judy in the back of the truck.

"I'll be a married woman the next time you see me," Judy declared at the bus station. I watched as Judy entered the station, openly flirting with the young soldier holding the door. I breathed a sigh of relief as she disappeared inside the building, and I could sense Nana and Gramps doing the same.

As Gramps started the truck, I looked seriously at Nana and asked, "If Judy marries Robert, will she be his cross to bear then?" All Nana could do was give me a big hug and let out a little chuckle. "I'm afraid, since I brought her into this world, that she will *always* be my cross to bear, dear."

Life on the farm was peaceful once Judy left. I got my stitches out in a couple of weeks, and Gramps said he thought the doctor sewed extra muscles in my arm, because I sure seemed a lot stronger. I never even ventured anywhere near the hog pen after that, and when Nana told me that bacon came from dead hogs, I relished it with a new vengeance.

Some of the ladies from church brought over clothes their girls had out grown, and it was like having all kinds of new presents. There was even a pair of pretty patent leather shoes in the offering, and I fell in love with them. Nana had me try them on, and even though my toes were squished up in the ends, I insisted they fit perfectly. Nana knew better, I think, but could tell how much I loved those shoes, so she said, "Well, it won't hurt if they're a little tight if you only wear them an hour or so on Sunday."

Every time I wore the shoes, they rubbed blisters on my heels and the tops of my toes, but I ignored the pain. I was going to church in pretty shoes, and that's all that mattered. Then, one day Nana noticed blood on my feet, and discovered the raw blisters festering there. She said that it was time for the shoes to find another little girl to make happy, but she promised me another pair just as soon as she could find one.

I would ride Freckles behind Gramps every evening while he did the chores. He told me I was a big help, because I could carry some of the grain buckets on Freckles, so Gramps didn't have to walk so far. I felt very important.

My feelings of importance and happiness would be dashed in a few days with the arrival of Judy back on the scene. She was blown in on the winds of pure evil, and the storm started as soon as she arrived. She had taken a bus from the City to town, and hitched a ride from town to the farm. I knew from the slamming of the car door and her "get out of my way" stride that it was not going to be a pleasant visit, but then again, was it ever? All I wanted to do was stay out of her way.

As soon as she came in the house, she stormed off to her room and slammed the door. We didn't see or hear anything out of her until Nana told her dinner was ready. She came out, and sat sullenly at the table.

She started eating before Nana had started Grace, but slammed her fork down when Gramps said something. After Grace, Judy sneered, "Well, aren't you going to ask why I'm not engaged?"

"I figured if you wanted us to know, you'd tell us. I know how cantankerous you get if I ask you anything. So, why aren't you engaged? I thought that young man couldn't wait to tie the knot."

"Well, I went to a party while Robert was on maneuvers, and some of his buddies told him about it. He got mad because I went, and said he didn't think I was ready to make a commitment to just one man. Can you imagine—getting that upset just because I went to a party? What did he expect me to do, sit around and twiddle my thumbs while he was gone?"

Nana gave Judy a cold, hard look. "What did you do at this party? Maybe that young man isn't so upset that you went to the party, but how you acted after you got there. Where you drinking and carrying on or what?"

"Why do you automatically assume it was from me drinking and 'carrying on'?" Judy yelled, angrily pushing her chair back from the table.

"Oh, I don't know—let me see…could it be the fact that you got yourself pregnant and had a baby by the time you were thirteen, or the fact that you run all over tarnation doing God only knows what to support yourself. I may not be educated, but you don't have to be a genius to figure out you're living a wild and shameless life. You should be trying to take care of Lizbeth instead of running after those GI's and going to wild parties!" Nana's face turned bright red as she bellowed the words to Judy. I had never seen Nana so angry.

"I could take care of Lizbeth if I had to, but why should? You took over that job as soon as you seen her--and I'm glad you did, 'cause I can't stand the little brat anyway!!" Judy's eyes glared with hatred as she spat out the words.

Nana looked at me, hoping I didn't comprehend what my mother was saying. The announcement of her hate for me was nothing I hadn't discovered long ago, but I couldn't understand why. Mothers were supposed to love their children. Nana loved Judy, even though she acted hateful. I didn't have any idea what I had done to make Judy reject me.

Judy once again went storming off to her room, slamming the door behind her. I felt as if the wind had been sucked out of me, but I was glad silence enveloped the room. No one ate very much of their dinner—the squabble had ruined everyone's appetite. Judy didn't come out of her room for the rest of the night, and I must say, I was happy she didn't! It took me a long time to get to sleep because I kept thinking what breakfast would be like. I wished Judy either go away again, or stay in her room forever!!

I awoke to a beautiful morning. The sun was peeping through the curtains, the rooster was proudly crowing, and I could smell the sharp aroma of bacon frying. I jumped out of bed, eager to take on the day—until I remembered Judy. The very thought of 'her royal grouchiness' put quite a damper on my sunny outlook, and added a sluggishness to my movements. Nana was calling me for breakfast, but I kept stalling as long as I good. Finally, the bedroom door was flung open, and Judy stood there, smiling and jokingly admonishing me, "Come on sleepy head—the day's a wastin' and your breakfast is getting cold!"

I stared at her in sheer shock for a few moments. She looked sort of like Judy. She was dressed in a pair of jeans and had her long, thick raven hair pulled back in a ponytail. Her face was scrubbed clean and showed no signs of 'war paint' (as Nana called it), her glowing skin radiating softness I had never seen before. It was as if some magic fairy God Mother had stolen into Judy's room and transformed her from some wicked, hateful witch into a beautiful and kind fairy princess.

Judy was bubbling all during breakfast. I saw Nana and Gramps both look at Judy in amazement every once in a while. She even told Nana to sit and enjoy her coffee while she cleared the table. I think Nana almost passed out. I hurried out to find Gramps, all the while waiting for the 'other shoe to fall.'

Later that morning, Judy found me in the barn with Freckles and a kitten I had gotten friendly with. "I'm going to go pick some wild flowers," she said. "Do ya want to come along? There's some beautiful ones over at the old Henderson place."

I looked at her guardedly. "Nana said I couldn't go there," I told her. "Well, not by yourself, silly goose! You're just a little girl. But you're going with me, and it will be ok. We're going to pick a beautiful bunch of flowers for Nana, and we'll make it an adventure, too. We can explore the old house. We might find a treasure!!"

There was a small voice inside my head that told me to stay put, but Judy made it sound like so much fun. And she was being nice to me. Maybe she had decided she liked me after all. If I didn't go—then she would stop liking me and be mad again. I pushed the little voice out of my head and took off down the road with Judy.

The Henderson place was a lot further on foot than it was by pick-up truck. We passed it all the time on our way to church or town, and it only took a few minutes to get there. Walking seemed to take forever, but Judy kept me entertained with stories about places she'd been and people she had met. We rounded a bend in the road, and there loomed the Henderson house.

The house had been empty for years, Judy told me. She knew the people who use to live there, but most of the family had moved away, leaving old man and old lady Henderson there alone. Then they passed away, but none of the family ever came back to claim the house. So it just stood there, rotting away day by day.

The house may have been rotting and shrinking away, but the yard was ablaze with the most beautiful blooms to be found anywhere. Long ago someone had put a lot of work and love into those flower gardens. I ran to what I thought was the most beautiful blooms, but Judy called after me, "Let's explore the house before we pick the flowers!"

Judy was waiting for me on the rickety front porch. "I know, let's play hide and seek in the house. I use to play with the kids that lived here—and there are the best hiding places in this house. I had one place where no one ever found me. I'll let you hide first, because when I hide in my secret place—you'll never find me."

My favorite game in the whole world was hide-and-seek, and I was very good at it. Nana said it was as if I rolled myself up in a little ball and became invisible. Judy cover her eyes and started counting, but I was a little hesitant to enter the house alone. It was big and dark, and kind of creepy.

"Why aren't you going in?" she asked. I just shrugged my shoulders. "Are you ascared? I'll go in the main hall with you, you big baby! You'll be okay once you see it's just a harmless old house, and then you can find a hiding place."

Judy pried open the old screen. One rusty hinge was all that was holding it on, and when Judy opened it, it laid back against the house at a weird angle. She took my hand in hers, and we walked into the old house. It was dusty and dirty, with spider webs hanging over the doorways. Judy swatted them down, and we explored from room to room. This was a nice house at one time, and I couldn't help thinking that with a little work, it could be nice again. Some rooms were in better shape than Nana's and Gramps house.

I had spotted some cabinets beneath some shelves in one of the rooms, and as soon as Judy covered her eyes, I ran and climbed in one of the cabinets, and quietly pulled the door shut. It was totally dark and musty smelling in the cabinet, but I didn't think it would be very long before Judy would find me.

As I lay huddled in the cabinet, I could hear Judy walking around, looking for me. She was saying, "I hope I find you before the wicked witch who lives here does. I've heard she likes to chop up little girls and put them in her stew."

I cringed as Judy called out the frightening words, hugged my knees close to my chest, and closed my eyes tight. Nana had always told me when I was scared, "Close your eyes tight, think of the Baby Jesus, and ask him to protect you. If you believe in Him, He'll protect you with his love."

I heard a lot of thumping on the other side of the door, and I thought that Judy or the witch one was trying to find me. I was too scared to play the game anymore, and all I wanted to do was let Judy know where I was at so she'd find me, but what if it wasn't Judy out there? What if it was the witch? I heard a scratchy rustling at the other end of the cabinet, and knew for sure the witch was sending her boogey man right through the cabinet walls. I held my knees tighter, squinted my eyes shut tight as they would go, holding my breath and praying all the while for Jesus to protect me with his love.

Suddenly a bright light filled the darkness, and a beautiful angel was wrapping her wings around me and singing softly in my ear. I felt like I was floating on clouds, drifting higher and higher into nothingness. Suddenly, I hear my name called. It sounded like Nana, but she was calling from far, far away.

The cabinet door flew open, and I plummeted back to my terrifying reality in a manner of seconds. I knew for sure the witch had found me, but I was determined to fight for my life, and when I saw hands reaching in the cabinet towards me, I started kicking and screaming with every ounce of strength I could muster. Then I heard Gramps saying, "Lizbeth, Lizbeth, it's me—Gramps. It's all right baby, I got cha."

Then my nostrils caught whiff of his earthy smell and I felt his work worn hands, and I knew it was really him. I was so happy to see him that I leapt into his arms, bumping my head on the top of the cabinet as I did so. I was trembling with fear, and crying tears of joy for being held in such strong, loving arms.

Gramps carried me out onto the porch, and let out a booming yell that he had found me. I was amazed to see that afternoon sunlight had dwindled into shades of twilight. I couldn't have been in that cabinet *that* long, but from what Gramps was saying, I had been gone long enough to have the whole countryside out looking for me.

Then, over Gramps' shoulder, I saw Nana bounding through the overgrown yard. She fell to her knees when she reached the porch, and Gramps sat me down, and I went running to her. First she gave me a hug so tight, I couldn't breathe. Then she grabbed both my shoulders and gave me a gentle shake. "What on earth got into you, child? You know you're not supposed to go out of the barnyard. What were you thinkin'? We've been worried sick, thinkin' a coyote or somethin' gotcha. Everybody's been looking for you for hours."

I started crying all over again. I was not used to Nana talking so harshly to me, and it crushed me to my very soul. In between sobs, I explained to Nana how I came to be there. I had just babbled out the part where Judy and I were playing hide-n-seek, when Judy wondered into the yard with Johnny Baker. Nana flew off the porch, grabbed Judy by her hair and started hitting her in the face, screaming, "You lying little bitch. You said you didn't know where she was, and you're the one that brought her here, and then left her. How would you have liked me to do something like that to you when you were her age? I swear, I believe the devil's took over your soul, you hateful little brat!!!"

I stood frozen in utter shock. I had never seen Nana raise her hand in anger, and I'd never seen her stand up to Judy. Gramps had to grab Nana's arms and pull her off Judy. Once separated from Nana, Judy looked around in amazement and embarrassment. Then she gave me a look of pure hatred as I cowered between Gramps and Nana. I had been on the receiving end of Judy's nasty looks, so they were nothing new to me. But the look that she gave me at that moment made me think she could squash me like a bug, and have no regrets.

Gramps had separated Judy and Nana, but Nana wasn't finished by a long shot. "You go back to the house, pack your bags, and get out!! I don't want to see you again until you make up your mind to live a decent life, and treat this child the way you should!! I've had it with your lying, hateful ways!!"

"With pleasure," Judy screamed back. "I can't wait to get out of this jerkwater town, and off your piss poor farm!" Then she turned to Johnny Baker, who had been frozen in amazement at the events that had transpired. "Johnny," she asked, "Will you take me to the bus stop?" All Johnny could do was nod, still in a daze. Judy took his arm, and he led the way to his beat up pickup. Judy got in and was practically sitting on Johnny's lap when he pulled off towards Nana's house.

It must not have taken long for Judy to get packed, because they sped past, heading towards town, as we were walking down the road towards home. Judy yelled something I couldn't understand, and then stuck her fist out the window with just one finger sticking up. I asked Nana what Judy was doing, and Nana said, "It's a new way of saying bye. Her finger was pointing towards Heaven, so she was saying she hopes we all go to Heaven."

I thought that was pretty nice of her, especially since she was so mad when she left. Nana had brought up the subject of Heaven, and that made me think of my angel. I told Nana and Gramps l was scared, and I did what Nana had told me to do, and the next thing I knew, I was in the arms of an angel. Gramps and Nana looked at each other kinda funny, and then Nana knelt down in front of me. She took both my hands in hers, and then quietly said, "Lizbeth, I have no doubt there are angels watching over you, but I think maybe you fell asleep, and was dreamin' about that angel."

Maybe Nana was right. Why would an angel visit me? But if it was a dream, it was the most beautiful and peaceful dream I'd ever had, and I couldn't wait to have it again!

It was early spring when Judy left, and summer was fading into fall when she came back. I turned four years old the first part of August, but Judy didn't come home for that. I didn't miss her, though. Nana and Gramps got me a pair of patent leather pumps for me to wear to Church, and they actually fit me. The Pastor gave me *The New Testament*, and I was thrilled to get it. I carried it to church with me, just like Nana carried her big Bible.

Nana had also made a new dress for me out of one of her dresses that she said was ready for the rag bin. I didn't see anything wrong with the dress, and it made a beautiful dress for me, and she made a matching one for my doll.

I had kept the box Robert had wrapped my doll in, and I kept it under my cot with my treasures in it—my doll and her dress, my shoes, and my little Bible. My new dress hung in the closet with Nana's. I would sit by my cot and play with my doll for hours, leaving the box open, because it also doubled as dolly's bed.

It was a rainy fall day, dark and gloomy. I didn't mind that I couldn't go out and play. It was a perfect day to play with dolly, and that's exactly what I was doing when there came a loud pounding on the door. I ran out to see who was there, because it was very rare to have company. Nana had opened the door to Sheriff Rollins, and he stood just inside the door, saying something softly to Nana. Nana turned real pale, and Sheriff Rollins helped her to a chair. I got to her side just as she started to cry.

"What's wrong, Nana?" I asked. I had never seen Nana break down and cry like she was right then. Tears welled up in my eyes, and there was a tremor in my voice. "Why are you so sad?"

Nana gathered me in her arms, burying her tears in the top of my head. I put my arms around her, and patted her back. In a few seconds, Pastor Thomas was at her side. Sheriff Rollins told Nana he had notified the Pastor on his way out, and hoped she didn't mind. Nana looked up, holding her hankie to her mouth and nose. "Thank you so much, Sheriff, for doing that."

Sheriff Rollins hung his head and said, "Sorry for your loss, Sadie.

Homer was a good man." Then he turned to leave, holding his hat nervously in his hands.

Now I was really confused. Nana hadn't lost Gramps, he just went to town. Pastor Thomas pulled up a chair next to Nana, and took one of her hands in his. "Sadie," he almost whispered. "Have you told Lizbeth yet?"

Now I was scared, because the news made Nana cry, and I was sure I would cry too. I wanted to climb inside Nana's heart to help it stop hurting. Nana shook her head at the Pastor and said, "I barely come to grips with it myself. I don't think I can put it into words just yet. Besides, you can probably explain it better than I could. Would you mind?"

Pastor Thomas pulled me up on his lap. "Lizbeth, I have something to tell you that's going to make you very sad, but then when I explain the beautiful side of it you'll feel a little better."

I looked into his face. His eyes were brimming with tears, and I knew the news was going to hurt, but I wasn't prepared for the utter destruction his words would have upon my heart. "Lizbeth, God called your Gramps home today. He's gone to be with God in Heaven."

"When's he comin' home?" I asked Pastor Thomas.

"That's the sad part, sweetheart. He won't be coming home ever again. He's gone to Heaven," Pastor Thomas gently replied.

The news that Gramps was gone, and would never be home again was impossible to understand. He loved me and Nana, so how could he leave us? "Why didn't he take us with him?" I cried to the Pastor.

Pastor Thomas searched for the words to make me understand death. "Your Gramps loved you and Nana more than anything in the world. He didn't want to leave you, but he had no voice in the matter. When God calls us, we have to go right then. But, your Gramps will be a special angel who will watch over you forever."

I angrily pushed away from Pastor Thomas, jumped off his lap and ran to Nana. "Nana," I cried. "You won't go to Heaven and leave me too, will you?"

Nana wrapped me in her arms and pulled me close. "Lizbeth, Sweetheart, I hope to go to Heaven *some* day, but not for a long time. I plan to be around to see you grow into a young lady."

Nana's words reassured me for the time being. I tried to imagine life without Gramps. Who would take care of the farm? Who would push me in the tire swing? He wouldn't be there to share his "when I was a boy" stories on those summer nights at the fishin' hole. My heart ached with missing him already. I wept silently for Gramps and eventually cried myself to sleep.

I awoke sometime later, still nestled in Nana's arms. I don't think she had moved a muscle. There were people milling around the house. Neighbor ladies and ladies from the church had heard the news, and were bringing food and telling Nana how sorry they were. Their husbands were busy doing the chores that me and Gramps and Freckles should be doing. *Freckles!* "I gotta tell Freckles. He'll wonder where Gramps is!" I told Nana as I climbed off her lap and headed for the door.

It seemed strange, wandering across the barn yard without Gramps' tall, lanky frame looming before me. I felt very small and very much alone right then. I quickened my steps to the barn, eager to see Freckles.

Freckles was in his lean-to, slowly munching on some hay. I opened the gate; telling Freckles, "I have to tell you something sad, Freckles. Gramps went to Heaven, and we don't get to see him again." I flung my arms around Freckles' neck, and the tears started gushing again.

I don't know what I expected Freckles to do. Do horses cry? Maybe he didn't understand what I told him, so I told him again. Freckles looked at me a couple of times, and then went back to munching his hay. I sat down inside the stall, and pulled my knees up tight against my chest. I rested my chin on my knees, closed my eyes and thought about Gramps.

"I wonder if he misses me as much as I miss him." I asked myself, half aloud. "I wonder what Heaven is like, and if he likes the angels more than me and Nana?" I ran these, and many other unanswered questions through my mind. I must have thought myself right into a dream.

Before I knew it, Gramps was standing right in front of me. I wanted to run to him, but I couldn't move a muscle. "Why are you so sad, Lizbeth?" Gramps asked in a musical voice.

"Gramps!" I cried, "They said you went to Heaven. I knowed you wouldn't leave me!"

"I am in Heaven, Lizbeth. God let me visit you one last time to tell you that I will always love you, and I will always be with you, even though you don't see me. You tell Nana that I love and miss you both. I left you my good luck piece under the rock at the fishin' hole. Don't cry—I'm in a beautiful place, and someday Nana and you will join me."

Then Gramps slowly faded into the blue haze that had filled the lean-to. Freckles whinnied off in the distance, but in a matter of seconds, he was standing over me, nibbling on my hair. I jumped up and excitedly asked, "Did you see him too, Freckles?! Gramps came to say good bye. I gotta tell Nana!!"

I raced across the barnyard, up the rickety porch steps and into the house, the screen door banging loudly behind me. "Nana! Nana!" I yelled, finding Nana at the kitchen table, nursing a cup of tea. "I saw Gramps!! He came to say goodbye, and he told me to tell you that he loves and misses us!"

"You must have had one of your dreams again," Nana said, as much to the other women in the room as to me. Then she spoke directly to them, "She has the most beautiful dreams, even in the daytime and then it takes forever to get her to see it wasn't real. This child has quite an imagination!"

The women, who at first had stared at me like I was crazy, nodded in understanding. Mrs. Henderson spoke up, "My Sally done the same thang. Don't fret none—she'll grow out of it!"

The ladies busied themselves fixing me a plate of food. "Come on, Child. You need to have some food," one of them said, while another guided me to the table.

I looked at the plate of food, and was almost sick. Then I looked at the ladies gathered around me, watching intently. "These nice ladies worked hard on fixing this food for us, so you go on and eat. Their feelins' a get hurt if ya don't," Nana said.

I knew that was Nana's way of letting me know that she'd be real disappointed in me if I didn't try to eat a little something as she winked at the other ladies. I forced myself to eat as much as I could, which was only a few bites, before I told Nana I didn't feel too good.

"You've had a hard, long day. Let's get you tucked in for the night," Nana said as she led me to the bedroom. She helped me pull my clothes off, and once I was snuggled under the covers, she sat on the side of the cot. "Lizbeth," she began. "You have got to watch telling people things like you saw Gramps or angels and stuff like that."

"But Nana, I really did see Gramps. He came to tell me bye." I didn't know how to convince Nana it was the truth.

"I think you just missed Gramps so much, and you wanted to see him so bad, that you just dreamed it. That's the wonderful thing about good dreams. Sometimes they seem so real, that it's hard to believe they're not. But the people around here are hard put to believe much about ghosts and angels, and such. It's a job for some of them to believe in God. They kinda feel if you can't touch or see it, then it ain't real. You have to live here, and you have one mark against you because your mother has a wild reputation. The fact that you were born on Friday the 13th is another mark. Some superstitious fools consider that a bad sign. Now, you can always tell me anything, but you have to be careful what you blurt out around other people. I don't want them to think bad about you."

I listened intently to what Nana was telling me. Why would someone think I was bad if I saw angels—angels are good things? But I made up my mind to keep my "dreams" a secret from everyone but Nana, just so she wouldn't worry. I drifted off into a fitful sleep while Nana told me the story of the *Five Loaves and Two Fishes.*

The next day, I remembered what Gramps had said about the present he had left me. I asked Nana if I could go to the fishin' hole, but she said she didn't have time to take me. So, I figured Gramps' present could wait a couple of more days—if it was there at all. I still hadn't gotten it right in my mind—had it been a dream or not?

There was always someone at the farm, helping with chores or dropping off food, or just visiting. Everyone was very nice, but I just wanted to be left alone. I spent a lot of time in the bedroom, playing with dolly or in the lean-to with Freckles. I missed Gramps so much.

The next day, after breakfast, Nana helped me get my Sunday clothes on. We were going to Church, and it wasn't even Sunday. Nana said we were going to "lay Gramps to rest."

"But Nana," I said, "I thought Gramps was in heaven."

"Gramps' soul went to heaven a couple of days ago, but we're going to put his body in the Church graveyard. Then we can visit his grave and leave flowers for him." Nana's eyes welled up with tears as she explained this to me.

I looked at Nana quizzically. "Why would we leave flowers?" I asked.

"People leave things that the person who is gone liked when they were alive. It's to show that you love and miss them."

"I know Gramps thought flowers were pretty—but he liked biscuits and gravy better. Maybe we should leave him that."The statement made sense to me, but Nana started laughing. I didn't understand why, but before I could ask for an explanation, there was a knock on the door.

Pastor Thomas had arrived to take us to the church. It was fun riding in a car, rather than a rumbling old pickup truck. When we arrived at church, Pastor Thomas led us to seats at the very front. There was a big box in front of the altar, with bouquets of flowers around it. The choir sang *Amazing Grace* and then Pastor Thomas started talking about what a good man Gramps was. Nana started to cry, and I leaned in close to her, not knowing what to do to help.

Pastor Thomas hadn't been talking long when the Church door was flung open by Judy, whose hair was a wild mess and her eyes were large and glassy. She steadied herself for a moment against the door, and then proceeded to zigzag her way down the main aisle. She flopped her body down in the pew next to Nana.

A hush fell over the congregation. Then a woman behind me whispered to the woman next to her, "I can't believe the little harlot would dare to enter the house of God!"

"What's a harlot?" I asked Nana, looking back at the woman as I did so. The woman blushed in embarrassment, and Nana put her finger to her lips and shushed me to be quiet.

Pastor Thomas started to speak again. It seemed like he talked forever, and then the choir sang *The Old Rugged Cross.* Then some of the men lifted up the box that Nana told me held Gramps, and started down the aisle towards the door. Then Pastor Thomas stood by the pew we were in, and waited for Judy to stand up. She nearly fell getting to her feet, but Pastor Thomas helped steady her. Then Nana and I followed.

We followed the men with the box out to the Church graveyard. There was a big hole in the ground, and after Pastor Thomas said a prayer, the men started to lower the box in the ground. Once it was in the ground, some other men started to shovel dirt on the box.

People gathered around Nana, who was crying softly. All of a sudden, there was a dull thump. When I looked around, there was Judy laying in a heap on the ground. "I think she's passed out," someone said. A couple of men picked her up and put her in Pastor Thomas' car.

On the ride home I heard Nana tell Pastor Thomas, "She reeks of booze. I hope everyone thinks she fainted because she was overcome with grief. I'm so embarrassed!"

"You have nothing to be embarrassed about," Pastor Thomas said. "We can't be responsible for the sins of our children."

When we got back to the farm, Nana and Pastor Thomas rousted Judy enough to get her into the bedroom. In a short time, the house was filled with more people, and *more* food. Nana explained that they were all friends and family who had come to pay respect to Gramps. I didn't have any idea what Nana meant, but I gathered it was a good thing.

I was standing by the lean-to, trying to explain to Freckles the flurry of activity on the farm, when Pastor Thomas came up and asked me if there was anything I needed. I studied him for a moment, and asked, "Can we go to the fishin' hole? That's where Gramps went to 'lax, so maybe he's there now."

"I suppose all this is a little hard for you to comprehend. I'll ask your Nana if it's all right for us to take a walk. We can have a nice talk on the way. Should we take a fishin' pole?"

I waited by Freckles while Pastor Thomas went to ask Nana. It would be nice if we found Gramps there, but deep in my heart, I knew he wouldn't be. But I would be able to look under the big rock and see if he left his good luck charm for me. It was just a few minutes before the Pastor returned saying, "Your Nana thought the walk would be good for you." He took my hand and we started down the path to the fishin' hole.

"You believe in angels, don't you?" I asked Pastor Thomas.

"Of course I do," Pastor Thomas answered. I looked up into his kind face. "Do you believe in ghosts?" I asked.

"Now, that's a hard one. I believe that when we die, our spirit goes to heaven or hell, and our body is returned to the earth. I can't say for sure if I believe in ghosts, as such. Why do you ask?"

"Just wonderin,'" I answered, as I shrugged my shoulders. "Nana believes in the Father, the Son, and the Holy Ghost. Do you?" I persisted.

"Yes, I do believe in the Holy Ghost?" Pastor Thomas stopped and bent down to look into my eyes. "Something's troubling you, child. What is it?"

"Nothin,' I was just wonderin," I answered, shrugging my shoulders again and kicking at the dirt. I continued, "If you believe in the Holy Ghost, then you believe in ghosts!"

Pastor Thomas chuckled, stood up and as we continued down the path, he said, "Lizbeth, I believe you're wise beyond your years. I'm not sure if that's a good thing, or a bad thing!"

We rounded a curve in the path, and there was the fishin' hole, set among trees decked out in their fall colors, and guarded by the big rock that Gramps and I would sit on to fish. The pond was crystal clear and mirror smooth, and the reflection of the fall colors across the water was breathtaking.

I broke loose of Pastor Thomas and ran for the rock, remembering the lazy summer afternoons we had spent there. I squatted down and felt in the dirt by the rock. I found it with no problem, as if an unseen force was guiding my hand. I pulled it out, blew the dust off it, and admired the large buckeye Gramps had carried in his pocket for as long as I could remember.

"What cha got there?" Pastor Thomas asked, catching up to me.

"It's Gramps. He told me it was here," I replied without thinking. Then I caught myself and added, "A long time ago."

Somehow I knew that this was one secret I had to keep to myself. After all—I didn't want people to think I was 'touched' as Nana would put it.

Judy was sick for the next couple of days, which suited me just fine. That only meant she would not feel up to making me miserable. But, unfortunately, she was up and about way too soon.

Nana or Judy either one spoke of what happened at the cemetery, and I knew it was best for me not to say anything either, although I was about to bust with questions. I certainly didn't want to stir up any kind of uproar, because Judy was being unusually kind to both Nana and I. I just figured

Judy hadn't regained enough strength from being sick to be her normal hateful self, but Nana said it was probably from feeling guilty.

I really hoped Judy was changing her ways, because when she wasn't being hateful, I could almost like her. She helped Nana around the house, and the two of us would do the chores right after breakfast. I was very guarded around her at first. I was very reluctant to be alone with her; after all, my previous experiences had conditioned me not to trust her. But, she seemed like a new woman, and I started to let my guard down a little.

One morning we were gathering eggs, and Judy asked me, "What do you want to be when you grow up, Lizbeth?"

I stopped dead in my tracks, my hand still clutching an egg in the nest. Was she really interested in me, or was she just passing time. I shrugged my shoulders and mumbled, "I dunno."

Judy kind of chuckled to herself and said wistfully, "I think when I was your age I dreamed of being a fairy Princess."

"Do you still want to be a Princess?" I asked; thinking to myself that she was beautiful enough to be one—at least as far as looks went. She was tall and thin, with thick raven hair that hung to the middle of her back. Her eyes where an emerald green, surrounded by dark thick lashes, and although she was only seventeen years old, she had the body of a grown woman. The features of her face were normally hard, with a chiseled appearance, but they had softened the last couple of days. "I must, 'cause I keep searching for Prince Charming. I keep coming up with frogs, though!"

"Do you have to marry a Prince to be a Princess?" I asked, finishing with, "How do you find a Prince?"

By this time we had made our way back to the house. Judy sat down on the top step of the porch, and motioned for me to sit next to her.

"You can't really become a Princess. We're poor, and higher class people consider us white trash. But I don't want to be like this all my life. I want to get out of this hell hole. I've seen what life can be like on the other side of the tracks, and that's what I want." Judy seemed to be talking more to herself than to me.

"What if a train comes when you're on the tracks?" I was thinking of Nana's warning to never go near the railroad tracks when I asked that.

Judy chuckled, got up, picked up the basket of eggs, and started in the house. It was starting to rain, and I was glad the chores were all done. I could spend the day with my treasures and enjoy the rhythm of the rain tapping on the roof. There were a couple of places that leaked, but Nana put big pots under them, so there was the tap-tap on the roof, with an intermittent plop-plop in the pots. Nana had settled into Gramps old easy chair, using this time to catch up on some mending, while the aroma of apple pie baking filled the house.

I went to the bedroom, took out my box of treasures, and began to play with dolly. Judy poked her head in the door. "You're awfully quiet. Thought I'd see what you were up to. What cha got there?"

"My treasures," I answered. Judy came over by me and peered into the box. "I guess your idea of treasures and mine are pretty different," she said with a sigh.

"Do you have treasures?" I asked. I had never seen her treat anything special, so I was curious.

"What makes something a treasure?" Judy asked.

"You know-- something that's special that you love. Dolly and my shoes and my Bible are special. Freckles is too, but he won't fit in the box. I love them all," excitedly sharing my treasures with her.

Judy looked at me like I was 'touched,' when I noticed she was all dressed up, wearing the war paint. I told her she looked pretty, and she said, "I have a date tonight, and I'll be leaving in a little while."

"Is it Prince Charming?" I asked my eyes wide with wonder.

"Lord, I hope so," she replied.

There came the loud blasts of a car horn, and I ran to the door to watch Judy leave in the fancy car that held a handsome man—who I hoped was her Prince. She no sooner got in the car, than it sped out of the barnyard, leaving a cloud of dust behind.

"Nana," I said excitedly, "Judy's going with Prince Charming!"

"We'll see," Nana said half-heartedly. "That girl needs to stop chasing fairy tales and grow up!" Nana seemed upset, but I didn't know why. Maybe she was just tired.

Nana heated up some stew she had made the day before, and we topped supper off with a piece of warm apple pie. We did the evening chores, and then Nana tucked me in, telling me the story of *David and Goliath*. It didn't take me long to fall asleep.

I was startled awake by a loud crash. I could see the flashes of lightning against the dark sky between the faded curtains, and thought that a tree had been struck. When the bedroom door swung open, and Judy stood there with her eyes blazing fire, I knew the real storm was raging *inside* the house.

She was at the cot in an instant, grabbed me by my hair, and pulled me up even with her face. Her eyes were wild and wide, and she spit as she slurred, "You snivellin' little brat. I wish to God you'd never been born!!" Then she tossed me across the room like I was a ragdoll. I hit the wall so hard, I saw little twinkle lights floating around.

Nana had jumped from her bed, trying to get to me, but Judy hit her so hard with her fist, that Nana's knees just buckled under her. Judy staggered towards me screaming, "I finally meet Prince Charmin,' and guess what—some bigmouth bitch tells him about you!!! Guess what—he don't want 'baggage' –which is you, you little piece of shit!!" I had rolled myself into a little ball, because I knew whatever contact we had was going to be painful, and I was right. She kicked me in the small of my back so hard it knocked my breath clean out of me.

Judy pulled her foot back to kick me again, but lost her balance and crashed to the floor, hitting her nose on my cot's iron headboard. Nana had managed to pick herself up, gathered me up in her arms and ran from the bedroom, grabbing the key to the old pickup on the way out.

Nana hunkered down to shield me from the pelting rain, but the wind was howling, and the rain was coming down so hard that we were both soaked by the time she got me in the truck. Nana tried to start the truck, but it just gave a couple of growls, and then died. She pumped her foot really hard, turned the key, and the motor roared to life. Nana put the truck in gear, and drove out of there like the devil himself was chasin' us. The old truck swerved from one side of the barnyard to the other, slippin' and slidin' in the mud.

I was shivering with cold and fear, wondering where we would go, but knowing it was best not to bother Nana with questions. We turned towards town, and in just a few minutes we turned into the lane to Pastor Thomas' house, who had a little house next to the church. The house was dark, but it was late, so the Pastor and his family were probably fast asleep. Nana pulled up as close to the house as she could get and then said to me. "Cuddle up next to me and try to get warm. I hate to wake the Pastor, so we'll try to tough it out here in the truck till daylight. About that time, Pastor Thomas was on his front step, flashlight in hand, yells, "Sadie, is that you out there?"

Nana jumped out of the truck, apologizing to Pastor Thomas, "Pastor, I'm sorry for wakin' you up. Judy's on a drunken warpath. She beat up on Lizbeth really bad, and even hit me. She has the strength of ten men when she gets like this. I just thought it would be best to get Lizbeth away before the dumb fool kilt her!!"Nana was breathless with excitement or anger—I wasn't sure which.

Pastor Thomas was holding the light with one hand, and pulling a suspender up over his shoulder with the other. He started down the steps and towards the truck, with Mrs. Thomas right behind him. "Sadie Cooper, you poor thing," she said to Nana. "you and that child get in the house this instant. You'll catch your death. We'll get you in some dry clothes and some hot tea down ya. You look like you're froze to the bone!!"

Pastor Thomas grabbed me up, and Mrs. Thomas hung onto Nana. Once we were in the house, Pastor Thomas said to Nana, "You got quite a shiner there!"

"I kinda figured I would. I tell ya, that girl scares me to death when she's all likkered up—it's like the devil himself has took over her soul!" The Pastor wrapped a blanket around Nana's shoulders.

Mrs. Thomas had begun to pull the wet nightgown over my head when she exclaimed, "My Lord, this child looks like she was trampled by a herd of wild horses!! She's got a goose egg on her head the size of a softball. You'd better call Doc Taylor and see if he thinks she needs to be looked at!!"

She wrapped a blanket around me, and as the Pastor picked up the phone, Mrs. Thomas started towards Nana. "Sadie, you come on here in the bedroom, and I'll get you some dry clothes. I'll get something for Lizbeth to wear, too."

Nana and Mrs. Thomas disappeared into the other room. I cuddled up in the blanket, in the Pastor's big easy chair and was about to fall asleep, when the Pastor shook my arm. "Come on, Honey. The Doc's on his way, and he said not to let you fall asleep, cause you could have a concussion."

About that time, Mrs. Thomas reappeared with a big shirt for me to wear, and a pair of socks that went all the way up to my knees. She rolled the sleeves up for me, and then carried me in the kitchen, placing me on a chair at the table. In a few minutes, Nana joined us. Mrs. Thomas put the teakettle on and told Nana what the Doc had said. Then she poured some milk in a pan and set it on a flame. The kettle started to whistle, and in a few moments, Nana had a hot cup of tea, and I had a cup of warm milk. "Don't know if the warm milk is a good idea or not. I don't want her to go to sleep, but I didn't think the caffeine would be good for her either," Mrs. Thomas said to Nana. She no sooner got the words out of her mouth, than a dog started barking, and there was a knock on the door.

Pastor Thomas opened the door to Doc Taylor, whose hair was rumpled, his shirt was hanging out, and his eyes looked heavy. He half mumbled greetings to everyone as he entered the kitchen, coming directly to me saying, "Now, let's have a look at this young lady."

He motioned to a side table there in the kitchen and asked Mrs. Thomas, "Do you mind if I sit her up here?"

"Not at all, "Mrs. Thomas answered, moving a couple of dishes she had on the table. Doc lifted me up, and then began prodding me all over, starting with the goose egg on my head. "You got quite a bump there," he said. Then, turning to Mrs. Thomas, asked, "Do you have an ice bag and some ice?"

"Yes, I do," Mrs. Thomas said, and started rummaging through a cabinet drawer. She got the ice bag ready and brought it to Doc. He placed it on my bump and asked if I could hold it there, while he continued looking me over. The ice seemed to help the pounding that was going on inside my head. After he finished looking me over, he lifted me off the table and back into my chair, sitting down next to Nana.

"Did Judy do this?" he asked Nana in a serious tone. Nana nodded, and he said, "Sadie, you're going to have to do something with that girl before she kills Lizabeth, or you, or you both!"

Nana hung her head, but not before I saw tears welling up in her eyes, saying, "I know—I just don't know what to do!"

Doc put an arm on Nana's shoulder and said, "I know this is difficult, but I think the best thing you could do for that girl is have Sheriff Rollins lock her up for a few days. She needs to realize she can't get away with this stuff. Lizbeth could very well have a concussion. There's not much we can do at this point—just keep a close watch on her for the next couple of days. Wake her up every couple of hours to make sure she's sleeping and isn't unconscious and I'll check on her in about a week or so. Are you going to stay here tonight?"

Nana shook her head. "No, I'm going back home. Judy should be passed out by now."

Pastor Thomas said, "Sadie, you're more than welcome to stay here. What if she's not passed out and still on a rampage? I'm inclined to agree with Doc. I think this is a matter for the Sheriff."

"I know you're right, but I'm just 'fraid it'll make matters worse," Nana lamented. "What happens when she gets out of jail? I know she'll be madder 'n a wet hen!"

"That's true," Doc Taylor said, folding his arms across his chest. "But, she'll get the idea that if she does this again, she'll go right back to jail. Judy maybe a drunk, but I don't think she's pickled that brain of hers yet."

"We'll all keep a close eye on you," Mrs. Thomas said, looking from the Pastor to the Doc. They both nodded in agreement.

"I suppose you're all right. Pastor, would you mind callin' the sheriff? The faster he can get here, the faster we can get out of your hair and let you all get some rest." Nana's voice was a hopeless whisper.

Pastor Thomas called the sheriff, and it seemed like he was there in no time. He sat at the table talking to Nana, writing something on a pad of paper every once in a while. I was having a hard time keeping my eyes open, so Mrs. Thomas laid me on their sofa. I didn't even wake up when they put me in the truck, or when the sheriff lifted me out when we got to the farm.

The sheriff and two deputies had followed Nana back to the house, which was dark except for one light in the front room, and eerily quiet. I woke up when Nana opened the door and exclaimed, "My Lord in Heaven, it looks like a twister set down here!"

I started squirming in the Sheriff's arms, and ran to Nana's side as soon as he sat me down. My eyes grew wide with amazement as I surveyed the total chaos in the house. Tables were turned over, dishes were broken on the floor, and Nana's sewing basket had been dumped and strewn about. I started to run in the house, but Sheriff Rollins stopped me. "Better let me go in first and make sure your mama ain't still on the warpath."

I wanted to scream, "She ain't my mama!" but thought better of it. Sheriff Rollins and the deputies went cautiously in the house. Pretty soon there was a real ruckus going on. Judy was screaming for them to get out and leave her alone, and I cringed at the sound of that voice. It took all three of them to handcuff her and drag her out of the house, but not before she managed to hiss, "I'll get you for this you little bitch!"

The deputies got Judy in one of the patrol cars and sped away. Sheriff Rollins came back in the house. "Do you want to press charges for her destroying your property?" he asked Nana.

"No, no point. Wasn't much worth anything no how," she answered back sadly.

I ran into our bedroom, and knew at a glance that Judy had destroyed all my treasures. Dolly had been torn apart, and her clothes were ripped to shreds, my shoes were nothing more than tattered pieces of leather, and the pages of my little Bible were ripped from the binding and strewn about the floor. I searched desperately under the debris, hoping to find Gramps' buckeye, but didn't find it anywhere. I sat down among the tattered remains of my precious 'treasures' and began to cry.

The next few days where a combination of joy and sadness. Judy had to do two weeks in the county jail, and it did my heart good to know that I would not see her during that time. I missed my treasures, and the time normally filled with pleasure from playing with dolly was now filled with hours of missing her.

Pastor Thomas gave me another little Bible, and one of the neighbor ladies gave me a pair of 'Sunday' shoes her little girl had outgrown. Once again I was wearing some else's cast offs that hurt my feet, but I wouldn't have told a soul—I was so happy to get them. Nana said that our friends and family was poor people, just like us, but they help out and give as best they can. Nana told me, "Don't matter if somethins' new or old—if it's give from the heart!"

Another lady gave me a doll she said she found in her attic. Her little girl was now grown up with a little girl of her own, but she wasn't big enough yet to play with dolls. I told the lady that when the little girl got big-I would give the doll back. She told me that that wouldn't be necessary, and Nana made my new dolly a couple of dresses—one for everyday and one for Sunday—just like me!

I never found Gramps' buckeye. I told myself that he must have needed it for a while, and come and got it while I was gone. I kept telling myself that he would bring it back someday, and I would look all around the big rock at the fishin' hole ever chance I got.

But, I still had Freckles. He was the most important thing in the world to me—besides Nana. I could tell him whatever I wanted, and know it would be a secret forever. I could tell him my hopes and dreams, and my troubles and fears. He would just nuzzle my cheek, or nibble my hair, as if to say everything'll be fine.

The sheriff dropped Judy by the farm when she got out of jail. He told Nana he used the ride as a good opportunity to give her a good talkin' to. "I told her she'd be staying a lot longer the next time she beats up on you or that little girl," he told Nana, and I was sure he meant it. His words made me feel a little more at ease, because I think Judy was afraid of the sheriff. She was ever so polite to him and Nana, and was even nice to me, saying, "I'm so sorry, Lizbeth! I just lost my head, and didn't know what I was doing. I promise I'll never do that again!"

I wanted to believe her, and pretended that I did, but somewhere deep inside; I knew she was just saying that because the sheriff was there. When he left, I thought for sure the angry hateful Judy would be back, but she was 'good as gold,' as Nana would say. I couldn't decide which would be better, having hateful Judy back and knowing to expect the worse, or this 'nice' Judy around, and not knowing what to expect—or when. I didn't trust her, and told Freckles not to trust her either.

Winter was upon us, and Nana came down sick. Doc came to the house to see her, and told Judy that she had "'monia", and would have to stay in bed and take medicine. Judy told Nana not to worry about anything, that she would take care of everything, including me. I was scared, but then I hear Nana telling Pastor Thomas when he came to visit, "It's like she's a changed person. I do believe the Lord's entered her soul. Goin' to jail did that girl a mess of good!"

Judy did the cookin' and cleanin,' and together we did the farm chores. At first I was afraid to go off with her by myself, but she never did anything mean, so I started to think Nana was right in what she told the Pastor.

Judy took care of Nana, too—feeding her broth, and wiping her forehead with a wet cloth. Nana didn't seem to be getting well. She coughed, but it was a dry, hacking cough, and she complained of her chest hurting so much she couldn't breathe. Nana told Judy how to make a mustard plaster, and Judy even let me help with it.

I got to stir the mustard seed powder, flour and egg whites in the bowl with a big spoon, until it got so thick I couldn't move the spoon. Then Judy spread the mustard stuff on a cloth, and put it on Nana's chest. Judy said it was important to have the cloth next to Nana's skin, and not the paste. The mustard plaster was only on a few minutes, and then Judy took it off. She said we would do another one after we did the chores.

Sunday morning, Judy took care of Nana, helped me get dressed, and then got dressed herself. She asked Nana if she would be ok by herself until we got back from church. I couldn't believe Judy was actually taking me to church, but she fired up the old pickup truck and away we went. Everyone in the congregation looked shocked as Judy and I walked in; after all, the last time Judy was in church was at Gramps' funeral, and she passed out.

After the service, Pastor Thomas asked Judy how Nana was doing. He said he would stop by later that afternoon to visit. Then he told Judy he was impressed with the changes she had made in her life, and hoped she kept on the right path. Judy looked uncomfortable with his words.

True to his word, Pastor Thomas and his wife visited Nana that very afternoon. She was still awfully sick, but told the Pastor that she didn't think she was ready to meet her maker yet. I didn't understand what she meant, but didn't ask any questions until Judy and I were doing chores.

We were giving Freckles some hay, and I asked Judy, "What did Nana mean when she said she wasn't ready to meet her maker?"

"Don't you know anything?" she replied, half annoyed. "She meant she wasn't ready to die yet."

I must have looked confused, because she added, "You know, like your Gramps."

"But Gramps went to Heaven," I said. "He's an Angel, and one day I'll see him again!"

"That's what they tell people when they lose someone, to make it easier," Judy replied.

My eyes began to well up, because what she said upset me so. "Gramps is not lost—he's an angel in Heaven!" It was the first time I had ever spoken angrily to Judy, and I regretted it as soon as I saw her eyes narrow into dark slits.

She raised her hand like she was going to hit me, and then changed her mind and lowered it, simply saying, "You believe what the hell you want, but truth of the matter is—your Gramps is dead and he's never coming back again! And, if Nana doesn't get better, she may be dead to!"

I was so upset by what she said that I didn't even stay to visit with Freckles. I went running to the house, tears streaming down my face, slamming the door behind me as I went in. Nana must have known something was wrong, because she called weakly to me.

I went to her bedside, trying to wipe my tears away, but when I saw her pale face and listened to her raspy cough, I couldn't keep the tears back. I blurted out what Judy had told me, and started crying all over again. She patted the bed next to her, and I crawled up beside her. "Don't you fret, child. Judy doesn't believe in angels yet, and probably not even Heaven. She can't see the good in this world, and that's what makes her so cantankerous. Lord knows, I don't want you to end up like her!"

Nana no sooner got the words out of her mouth, when I looked over and saw Judy standing in the doorway, her face screwed up in a vicious stare aimed directly at me. Nana spotted her too, and told me, "You'd better say 'night to Freckles before it gets too late."

I started towards the door, but didn't walk to fast, wanting to listen to what was said. Nana said to Judy, "What in the world is wrong with you, upsetting the child like that!!" The effort was too much for her, and she started coughing long and hard.

"Come on, Ma!" Judy replied. "You can't be filling her head full of fairy tales about Angels and such. She needs to learn what life is all about! And just why are you so afraid that she'll be like me? Am I so damn bad? Who the hell's been doing all the work around here the last few days?"

Nana sounded so tired and weak when she answered back. "She's only four years old. Let her be a little girl. She misses her Gramps, and I tried to make things easier on her. She doesn't understand what death is all about. I just don't want her to grow up bitter and angry at the world, like you are. I know you've been doing everything around here, and I appreciate it. But that gives you no call to be hateful to Lizbeth."

I had made it out to the porch when I heard Judy say loudly to Nana, "That little brat is all you care about anymore. You better remember one thing—she's *my* daughter—not yours!"

Nana barely got out "Then start acting like her mother!" before she started on another coughing fit. I ran out to tell Freckles what I had heard, and to let him know that I thought the old Judy was on her way back.

When I went back in the house, Judy was all dressed, with her war paint on, telling Nana she was taking the truck and going to town, and that her precious Lizbeth can do for her if she needs anything. Nana gave her a look that even I understood. It said, "Don't come home drunk." Judy headed out, slamming the door behind her. I heard the old truck fire up and roar away.

Judy didn't come home for three days. I tried to do for Nana as best I could the first day, but I don't think it was good enough. Nana tried to get up in the afternoon, but she was too weak. I didn't know what to do. I knew I wasn't suppose to go away from the farm by myself, but I knew I had to do something to help Nana, so on the second morning I told Nana I was going to do chores. Then I started down the road as fast as I could to the Johnsons, who were our closest neighbors.

It seemed like it took forever for me to get there, and I was short of breath from running when I knocked on their door. Mrs. Johnson was surprised to see me, and I breathlessly told her about Nana. Mrs. Johnson said, "I knew your Nana was sick, but I thought Judy was taking care of her."

I quickly explained the argument Nana and Judy had and that Judy left and hadn't been back. Mrs. Johnson told her oldest girl, Kate, to mind the kids, and then hollered for her husband to take us to Nana's. Her husband drove faster than I'd ever rode before, and I was bounced all over the truck, but I was glad he was going fast because I wanted to get back to Nana.

Once there, Nana was surprised to see Mrs. Johnson, and when she told Nana I had run all the way to their house to fetch her, Nana tried to look mad, but I could tell she really wasn't. Mrs. Johnson busied herself fixing food and applying mustard plasters. She gave Nana a sponge bath and combed her hair, and Nana said that it made her feel so much better.

Towards evening, Mrs. Johnson said her husband would bring Kate when he came, and Kate could stay the night. Mrs. Johnson told Nana she would be back in the morning, but Nana tried to protest, saying it was too much on Mrs. Johnson. "After all," Nana said, "You have your own family to take care of."

"Now you hush up," Mrs. Johnson told Nana. "You and Homer helped us out many times. Now I have a chance to repay you."

Before long, Mr. Johnson came to take his wife home, and leave his daughter behind. Kate was a stout girl, but had a very pretty face. She was a year older than Judy, and a lot more fun. We did the chores, and then we played a couple of games. Kate taught me how to do 'cat-n-cradle.' After supper, she read me a story, and tucked me into bed. She made a pallet next to Nana's bed on the floor. I went to sleep wishing Kate was my mother instead of Judy.

Early the next morning, Mrs. Johnson was there, as promised. I hated to see Kate go, but she promised she would come visit me real soon. Nana seemed to be doing better, so much so, that Mrs. Johnson helped her get out of bed and into Gramps easy chair. She was not having as much trouble breathing, and kept saying how much better she felt.

It was the middle of the afternoon when Judy returned to the farm, in her usual hateful frame of mind. I could tell by the way she drove the truck into the barnyard, came to a screeching halt, and slammed the door when she got out. She had an angry scowl on her face and when she saw Mrs. Johnson, she asked, "What the hell are you doing here?"

"Don't you use that tone with me, young lady, or you'll be talkin' out the other side of your mouth! I came to help your Ma and Lizbeth. What got into your head—leaving a four year old alone with a woman as sick as your Ma? When you were younger, everyone talked about how smart you were, and now, I swear, you don't have the sense God gave a goose!"

Mrs. Johnson was wagging her finger in Judy's face the whole time she was talking, and while Judy looked like she wanted to rip that finger right off Mrs. Johnson's hand, she didn't move a muscle. All she did was give a sarcastic "Are you finished?" when Mrs. Johnson stopped talking. Then she turned in a huff, marched off to her room and slammed the door.

Mrs. Johnson said to Nana, "I swear, Sadie, I don't know how you put up with that girl!! I would have beat her half to death by now!"

"I never hit the girl, and maybe that's the problem," Nana told Mrs. Robinson. "She was a pretty good girl, up till her father died. I thought she adjusted pretty good, but then when I married Homer, she just went wild. Homer never gave her no call to dislike him, so I never could figger what her problem was."

"You know, you can raise 'em so big, and then their own mind takes over. Who knows the whys and wherefores of why a body acts the way they do. Maybe she was just a 'bad seed' and the meanness just laid quiet for awhile." Mrs. Johnson was brushing Nana's hair as she spoke, and every once in a while, Nana would nod in agreement.

Mrs. Johnson cooked up a bunch of food, saying, "This should hold you for a few days." Mr. Johnson came to get his wife in the late afternoon, and he had brought Kate with him. I heard her tell her husband that Kate won't need to be staying the night because the 'little heathen' had come back home. Then she bent down to me and said, "Lizbeth, if you need us for anything, and I mean *anything*, you scurry over and fetch us, ok?!"

Judy came out of her room after Mrs. Johnson left. We all ate supper, and then Judy told Nana, "We need to get you back to bed. You look tired as can be."

She helped Nana to her bed, gave her medicine, and then said to me, "We need to get them chores done."

I went out the door ahead of her, and didn't notice Judy was carrying Gramps hunting rifle until we got to the lean-to. "Why you got that?" I asked, pointing to the gun.

Judy, ignoring my question, said, "You know, this last mess with Ma happened 'cause you don't know what 'dead' is. Ma fills your head with stories of angels, and heaven, and all that nonsense. But, I'm your mother, and I think you should know the truth of life and death."

With that said, Judy raised the rifle and pointed it at me, I thought.

When I heard the loud crack of the bullet, I realized it wasn't me the gun was pointed at, but Freckles. The bullet struck him right between the eyes, and he went down with a loud thump. I ran to Freckles, kneeled beside him, telling him to get up. He just laid there, blood oozing everywhere. I put my arms around his neck, screaming his name, feeling his warm, sticky blood seep through my dress. As I cried hysterically, Judy walked over beside me and calmly said, "That's what dead is.

I was heartbroken over losing Freckles. It seemed like I had lost everything that I loved except for Nana, and I didn't like to let her out of my sight. I was afraid that she might disappear from my life also.

Nana was furious with Judy for shooting Freckles. She told Judy it was a disgustingly selfish and childish thing to do, and she wanted her to leave. She told Judy she could leave on her own, or she would have Sheriff Rollins drag her off the farm. Judy left on her own that very day.

It was nice not having to worry about Judy, and what terror she would subject me to next, but it was a very lonely life for me. My best friend was no longer there to pass the hours with, and he wasn't there to hear my secrets. Some of the neighbor men had heard what happened and they came to bury Freckles for me. We placed a wooden cross over his grave, and I would go there often to visit. I often wondered if he was in Heaven with Gramps, or did animals go to a different Heaven?

Nana said they were very worried about me after Freckles died. I wouldn't eat or speak, and wouldn't get out of bed for three days. I didn't want to tell Nana that I had gone to my 'special place.' I wasn't sure she would understand the place I went when I was hurting so bad. In this place, my pain was eased, and I could be with the ones who I loved, and who loved me. To Nana it would have been a dream world; a place of make believe. For me it was an escape from my life of pain.

But, I couldn't stay in my special place forever, and had to leave it to come back to life on the farm. I became aware of Nana crying at my bedside, begging me to return, and through the gray fog of the other world I knew I had to return for her sake. In a few days I was back to normal as far as anyone could tell.

The work on the farm was hard on Nana. I tried to help as much as I could, but I was only four years old, so I know I didn't replace Gramps. Some of the neighbor men would stop by to help with the heavy stuff, and when Nana offered to pay them what little she could, they would refuse to take it, saying, "That's what neighbors are for." So, Nana would make them a pie to show her appreciation.

Winter was rearing its ugly head, and Nana had canned for days on end so we would have food during the winter. Nana said, "We have to be like the squirrels and put food away for hard times."

I loved helping in the kitchen. Nana would let me stand on a kitchen chair so I could reach the bowls and pots and pans. She said I stirred better than anyone she knew. She said when the time came, we would make Christmas cookies. I loved Christmas cookies, and this would be my first time making them.

Life was busy and by no means easy, but I loved sharing it with Nana. She called me her little shadow, because wherever she went, I was right behind her. If truth be known, I didn't want to let her out of my sight. She was all I had left, and what would I do if anything happened to her?

One day the mailman brought a letter to Nana. It was a pretty big deal, 'cause we never got any mail to speak of. All our family and friends lived close by, so there was no reason to send letters. I was excited as Nana closed the door and tore open the envelope. As she read the letter silently to herself, she got a sad worried look on her face. "What's wrong, Nana?" I asked.

She sat heavily in her rocking chair, laying the letter on the little table beside her, and drew me up on her lap. "That letter is from your mother," she started saying. "She got married a couple of days ago, and they want you to come live with them. They will be here in a few days."

I jumped off Nana's lap and let out a powerful. "No! I don't want to live with Judy! I don't want to leave you, Nana! She can't make me, can she?"

Nana looked thoughtful for a moment, and then said (more to herself than me), "Gramps and I adopted you when you were just a baby. So, legally, she can't make you go with her. I can't understand her sudden interest in you now. We'll just have to wait and see."

I was hoping the days would crawl by, waiting for Judy to come. Instead, they flew by, and I clung to Nana more than ever. I was afraid I would have to go with Judy, and I was afraid of what my life would be like if that happened. Judy was mean to me even when Nana and Gramps were around to protect me. I hated the thought of what she would do if I was all alone with her.

It was a cold December day when a fancy car pulled into the barnyard. A tall, lanky man got out from behind the wheel, went around, and opened the passenger door. Judy got out, and came running up on the porch, throwing her arms around me, and giving me slobbery kisses. "Oh, sweetheart! It's been so long since I saw you. My but you've grown. I have a surprise for you—I brought you your new daddy!"

I pushed myself out of her grasp, and ran behind Nana, not bothering to hide my surprise or dislike of Judy, and the whole situation in general. I watched as the young man reached into the backseat of the car and brought out two grocery bags, and then slowly make his way to the porch. "Cliff, this is my mother, Sadie. Hiding behind her is my daughter, Lizbeth. Mother, this is my husband, Clifton Sweeney. He's in the Air Force."

The man sat the bags in a chair on the porch, and reached out to take Nana's hand. In a rich, powerful voice he said, "It's a real pleasure to meet you, Mrs. Cooper."

"Let's get in out of the cold," Nana nervously said. "And, since you're married to my daughter, we don't need none of that Mrs. stuff. Just call me Sadie. You're family now."

Everyone went in the house. Nana had a fire going in the pot bellied stove, and the house was nice and warm. The man tried to talk to me, but I clung to Nana's dress, peeking out at him every now and then. He said to Nana, "We brought these groceries, because I didn't think it right us just showing up without some contribution to the cause. Judy has some gifts for you all out in the car. Lizbeth, would you like to help me carry them in?"

I looked at Nana for some indication as to what I should do. She said, "Go ahead, Lizbeth. Help Cliff fetch their things."

On the way to the car, Cliff said, "I'm really anxious for you to come live with us. We'll have a nice house, and you can have your own room and everything."

I stopped dead in my tracks and asked him, "Can Nana come too?"

"I don't think your Nana will want to leave the farm forever, but she is welcome to come visit you at anytime," was his reply.

"I don't want to go. I'll stay with Nana!" I said in a determined voice.

Cliff handed me a box that wasn't very heavy, but almost as big as me to carry in, and he loaded a few boxes in his arms asking, "Can you handle that ok?" It was awkward, but I didn't want him to think I was a baby, so I nodded yes, grasping the box tightly. "I'll get the suitcases later," Cliff said as we headed towards the house.

Once back in the house, I took off my coat and sat next to Nana. Judy was in the kitchen, unpacking the groceries and starting dinner. I kept looking at her, expecting the Judy I knew to make an appearance. The Judy that was there now was someone I didn't recognize at all. She looked the same, but it was like someone nice had possessed her, and I expected that other person to leave at anytime, and the real Judy to show up.

In a little while, we all sat down to eat. Judy said to Nana, "We've rented a nice little house not far from the base, and Lizbeth will have her own room. We bought her new furniture, and I'm sure she'll like it. There's a family living next door that has a little girl about her age, so she'll have someone to play with."

I blurted out, "I want to stay here!" without thinking. I looked at Judy defiantly, feeling safe in Nana's presence. Judy narrowed her eyes into small slits and stared into my face. There she was—the Judy I knew, but she was only there for a moment. Judy gave me a smile and said, "We can work out the details. I'm sure you'll change your mind, Lizbeth, when you realize how nice things will be for you. The presents we brought are just the beginning."

Nana said, "You know, Judy, I have custody of Lizbeth. If she doesn't want to leave, I can't see forcing her. Maybe she could just visit for a short time to see how she likes it."

Judy's eyes narrowed again, but this time the evil stare was directed at Nana. She started to say something, but then she just smiled, shrugged her shoulders and said, "We'll see."

After we finished eating, Judy told Nana and I to open our presents while she cleaned up the kitchen. Cliff handed me the large box I had carried in, and told me to open it. I untied the ribbon that was around the box, lifted the lid and was amazed at what I found inside. There was a doll in a beautiful red dress, with white patent leather shoes, lacy socks, and golden hair. She was beautiful. I'm sure Cliff could tell I was delighted, and he quickly showed me that if I laid her down, her eyes would close, and she would cry. When I stood her on the floor, she was almost as big as I was, and I could make her walk, too. I was sure she was the most beautiful doll in the world. I asked Cliff what her name was, and he said, "the name on the box is 'Saucy Walker,' but I think that's the brand name. You can name her anything you want."

Thinking back to the doll I had once had, I said, "I'll call her Dolly."

"That's a good name," Cliff said. I couldn't help but like him. He had a gentle smile and manner that put me at ease. "There's more," he said, handing me a large sack. He also handed one to Nana. Inside my sack was two new dresses, and a brand new coat. Nana had a new coat and hat in her bag. She thanked Cliff, and so did I.

"There's one more bag," Cliff said excitedly, handing me another large bag. Inside was some pretty little panties, some lacy socks, like Dolly's, a new flannel nightgown, and in the very bottom of the bag was a pair of black leather snow boots and a pair of patent leather slippers. Cliff laughed as I squealed with delight. "Your mother said you would like those," Cliff said between chuckles.

I looked at Judy, and she was smiling at me. She had softness in her eyes I had seen only on rare occasions, and I wondered if she was trying to make up for my 'treasures' she had destroyed. Perhaps so, but past experiences had taught me well—I still didn't trust her.

The excitement of the day caught up with me, and I began to yawn. Judy helped me put on the new night gown, and tucked me into bed, Dolly lying beside me. She even read me a story. I asked Judy, "Is Cliff your Prince Charming?"

"Yes, Lizbeth, I do believe he is. And I think you should get used to calling him 'Daddy,' because that's what he is now."

I drifted off to sleep with thoughts of a wicked witch who had married a Prince, and had turned into a beautiful Princess.

The next morning at breakfast, Judy started talking about what my life would be like if I went with her and Cliff. I slammed my spoon into my oatmeal and said defiantly, "I'm staying with Nana!"

Cliff chuckled and said, "I see she has her mother's temper."

"Lord, let's hope not!" Nana said.

Judy was shocked at my outburst, but simply smiled and calmly said, "I tell you what, Lizbeth, after breakfast, you get dressed, put on your new coat and boots, and you and I will go for a walk and have a nice talk. When we get back, if you still want to stay with Nana, then that's what you will do, ok? While we're out, we'll look for a nice Christmas tree."

I thought Cliff would be going for the walk too, and was scared when I discovered it would just be me and Judy. I had a bad feeling deep in the pit of my stomach, and tried to think of a reason not to go. But, when we came back, if I still wanted to stay with Nana, Judy said I could, and I knew I wouldn't want to leave her. It seemed like an easy way to stay, so Judy and I set out towards the woods.

Back in the woods, not too far from the house, was a bridge made out of wood and rope. It stretched across a deep ravine, and the bridge was a short cut to get to the other side. Nana and I had crossed on the bridge many times during the summer to get to her favorite blackberry patch. While Judy and I walked, she described all the beautiful things I would have if I went with her and Cliff. "Before long, you'll be starting school, and military kids go to good schools. Also, you'll get good medical and dental care. I know that doesn't mean anything to a kid, but Nana can't afford the Doc to see after you. If you love Nana so much, then you should think what's best for her. She's getting too old to look after a kid. Her life would be much easier if you weren't here."

By this time we were halfway across the bridge. I told Judy, "Nana loves me and wants me with her. She's told me so."

With no warning, Judy picked me up and held me head first over the rope rail of the bridge. All I could see below was rocks and trees, and a small stream. I was terrified, and as the blood rushed to my head, I heard her say, "You know what dead is. I could let go right now, and you would be dead, and everybody would think it was a terrible accident. But, I need you alive. I'll get more of an allotment with a kid. So, I promise you right now, if you don't go back to the house and act like you want to come live with me—I'll kill Nana. Then you won't have anybody. Is that what you want?"

I screamed, "No, No—don't hurt Nana! I'll go! I'll go!"

With that, Judy lifted me back on the bridge, but she grabbed hold of my hair and pulled viciously. "Don't even think about telling anyone about this, or Nana's dead for sure—you understand?"

I couldn't stop trembling, and tears were rolling down my cheeks.

I slowly nodded, and Judy said, "Stop that damn sniveling before we get back to the house. You screw this up for me, so help me, you'll be sorry! And another thing, I'm your mother, so you'd better call me Mama, or I'll tan your hide!"

I would rather eat dirt than think of her as my mother, but I was terrified for Nana. Judy was evil enough to carry out her threats, and that knowledge left me no choice but to do as she demanded. On the way home, I convinced myself that I could tell Nana the lie (something I hated to do) about wanting to live with Judy. Nana's life depended on it.

When we got to the house, I walked in and sadly sat by Nana. "What's wrong, Lizbeth?" she asked.

Tears welled up in my eyes, and my voice quivered as I said, "I don't want to make you sad, Nana, but I think I want to live with Ju—Mama."

Nana looked shocked, I don't think so much by the fact that I wanted to live with Judy, but by the fact that I had called her 'Mama.' Judy had never wanted me to call her that before, and I never really thought of her as my mother, so it was easy not to.

Nana put her arms around me and hugged me tight, saying, "I want you to know that I love you more than anything, and I will miss you like the dickens when you're gone, but Cliff and I had a long talk while you two were walking. He's in a position to give you a much better life than I can, and an education. So, I think you made the right decision. And, Cliff says he will bring you to visit. As a matter of fact, in a few weeks he's going to take some leave and come back here and help me sell this old farm. Then I can get a little house in town and not have to work so hard. So, you'll be coming back in a few weeks!"

Well, it seemed everything had been decided. I cried myself to sleep that night, knowing that in just a couple of days I would pack up what belongings I had and leave with a woman who hated me and a man I didn't know.

It would take 4 hours for us to reach the town outside the Air Force Base where Cliff was stationed, but to me it seemed to take forever. I spent a lot of the travel time escaping to my special place. Seeing Nana standing on the porch, tears streaming down her face broke my heart. Nana was poor, and may not have been able to afford the luxuries of life, but she made that up with boundless love and understanding. I was scared to face life with Judy, unsure of what my treatment would be. I knew that Judy didn't love me like Nana did, and her motherly instincts did not go beyond her own wants and needs.

Cliff tried very hard to put me at ease, reassuring me often that I would be happy. When we finally arrived at our new home, he carried me into the house, excited for me to see my very own room, and the boundless toys and clothes that were for me. He introduced me to the neighbors as his daughter, and I couldn't help but get the feeling that he was glad I was there. I couldn't help but like him, and I called him Daddy with ease. I felt safe and protected when he was around.

Two days after we arrived at the house, Cliff kissed me goodbye, explaining he had to go to work. He was dressed in a brown uniform, and he looked very handsome to me. I could understand why Judy thought of him as her Prince. I really didn't want him to leave, because this would leave me alone with Judy for the first time since we were on the bridge. My insides were shaking with fear.

Judy had gotten up and made breakfast, and as soon as she kissed Cliff goodbye, and he backed the car out of the driveway, Judy turned to me and said, "We're going to get the housework done, and then we're going out. You're going to help. You can start by making your bed and straightening things up."

I did the best I could to please her, but the bed wasn't made perfectly, and she pushed me across the room as she rushed past me, yelling, "This bed looks terrible. Cliff will know right away I didn't make it. I'm going to show you how, and I expect you to do it right from now on!"

After showing me how to do different chores around the house, she told me that they were things she expected me to do every day. Then she told me to get dressed, that we were going to take a bus into town. I did as she said, and then we quickly walked the block to the bus stop.

I was excited as the big bus pulled up to the stop. I had never been on a bus before, and I knelt on the seat, so I could look out the window. The city was much different from the little town I was use to, and I was absorbing the sights and sounds like a sponge. It was all new and exciting.

At one of the stops, a young soldier got on the bus and sat across the aisle from me and Judy. He started talking to Judy right away, and when he asked about me, she explained that I was her daughter. I got the feeling that they weren't strangers when he said to Judy, "I didn't know you had a kid." Then he asked where we were going. Judy told him that we were going to do some shopping. He asked if he could buy Judy a drink when we were finished, and Judy agreed to meet him at two o'clock.

We got off the bus in a short time and went into the biggest store I had ever seen. It was like a fairy tale, with all kinds of twinkly lights, and *Away in a Manger* music filling the air. The store was crowded, and people were rushing around. Judy said they were Christmas shopping, and that's what we were doing too. Judy stopped at one counter, picked up a bottle, and sprayed smelly stuff all over her and me both. The smell was so strong it took my breath away. Judy said it was perfume. She bought a couple of things, looked at her watch, and said we had to leave.

We walked a couple of blocks to another store, but Judy said it was a restaurant, and they sold food and drinks. The soldier from the bus was already there, seated at a table with a glass in front of him. He stood up when we walked towards the table.

He hugged Judy and gave her a kiss, and for some reason, I felt that was wrong. Judy had said he was just a friend, but friend or not, I decided I didn't like him. He said something to a young woman, who came to the table, and she left but came back in a few minutes with a glass of something (like his) for Judy, and something Judy called an Ice Cream Soda for me. I had to get on my knees to reach the table, but the stuff in the glass tasted so good, I wouldn't stop sipping on the straw until I got a terrible pain over my eye. Judy and the soldier laughed when I complained about the pain.

After a few minutes Judy said, "Lizbeth, I'm going to the bathroom. Do you need to go?"

I shook my head, preparing to attack the soda again. When she was out of sight, the soldier moved his chair towards me, placing his hand on my arm. "You know, Lizbeth, you're a very pretty young lady," he said, rubbing my arm softly.

Feeling very uncomfortable, I pulled away from him, mumbling a shy "thank you." Once again I told myself I did not like this man. His breath was sour, and I didn't like him touching me. He scooted his chair back where it was when he saw Judy coming towards us. Judy sat down, saying, "Finish your soda, Lizbeth. We have to get home." The soldier and Judy agreed to meet the next day at the same time.

On the way home, Judy told me not to say anything about the soldier to Cliff. When I asked why, she squeezed my cheeks together hard with her hand and between clenched teeth said, "Because I said so and that's the only reason you need!"

When Cliff came home that evening, he gave Judy a kiss, and sat down at the table for dinner. He looked at me and asked, "What did my two ladies do today?"

I looked at Judy, unsure what I should answer. She quickly told Cliff, "We took the bus into town and did some Christmas shopping, and then we stopped and we had and ice cream soda."

I knew then what it was safe to talk about, and excitedly told Cliff about the bus ride, and how good the ice cream soda was. He chuckled at my excitement, and then asked, "Have you written to Santa yet to tell him what you want for Christmas?"

I was puzzled, and the look on my face must have told him so. Judy explained to him that Nana never made a big fuss over Christmas, because she couldn't afford much. Cliff nodded in understanding, and then said to me, "Well, this year Christmas is going to be big. I will help you write a letter to Santa, and you can tell him what you want, and we'll get that in the mail to him."

Later on that evening, Cliff and I sat at the kitchen table, and he did indeed help me write a letter to Santa. When he asked me what I wanted for Christmas all I could think of was to say, "I want to see Nana."

I had more material things than I'd ever had in my life, but I missed Nana something awful, and I wanted to see her more than anything. Cliff laughed and said, "You can ask Santa for something just for you. We're going to see Nana in two weeks. We're going to help her move, so you'll get to see her for 3 or 4 days. Maybe we can get her a telephone like we have, and then you can call her once in a while."

I was so happy with the prospect of seeing Nana again, that I forgot myself and threw my arms around Cliff's neck and gave him a big hug. He hugged me back, and then said, "So, what do we ask Santa for now that you know you'll see Nana?"

I didn't have any idea what to ask for, so I just shrugged my shoulders. Cliff said, "We have time, so why don't you think about it for a few days, and you can get some ideas when you and your mom are shopping in town, ok? Then we'll finish the letter to Santa."

When Cliff tucked me in latter, I drifted off to sleep with happy thoughts of seeing Nana soon, and thinking that Judy was right—Cliff really was a Prince Charming. The telephone Cliff had talked about was a magical device that lets you talk to people miles away. I couldn't wait to tell Nana about such a device.

Every day for the next week, I would get up, do the house hold chores, and as soon as Cliff left for work, Judy and I would take the bus into town. Every day, Judy would meet the young soldier at the restaurant.

One day, Cliff came home from work and said he was going to have to go out of town for a few days—the government was sending him somewhere. He told Judy he would leave the car for her, so we wouldn't have to take the bus if we wanted to go anywhere. I was disappointed because Cliff would be gone, and I enjoyed the bus rides into town. That night Judy helped Cliff pack a bag, and a car was at the door bright and early the next morning to pick him up. Cliff gave me a big hug and kiss goodbye and told me to be a good girl. I hated to see him leave.

The next day, Judy told me we wouldn't bother cleaning the house that morning, we were going to town early. We got dressed, and left in the car. Judy drove to town and parked in a parking lot, and we went in the store for a little while. Then, she got in a box with windows in it, took some coins out of her purse, and told me she was going to talk to someone on the telephone. I stood outside the box and waited. When she was done, she came out and said we were going to a party.

We got in the car and Judy drove for a little while around the city streets. Before long she stopped in front of a rundown house. We went inside. There were a lot of people inside. They all spoke to Judy, some of them hugging her and laughing and joking. Blaring music and cigarette smoke filled the house, along with a sour musty smell.

Judy took me over to a large man sitting on a tattered couch. He had on a dingy white undershirt, and smelled of beer, cigarettes, and sweat. He was unshaven and had foul breath and yellowed teeth. Judy told me his name was Jake, and he was the owner of the house. She told Jake I was her little girl, and my name was Lizbeth.

Jake gave Judy a sly smile, and said, "Now Judy, you just leave Lizbeth with me. I'm sure we'll become good friends. You go and have a good time. I've got some friends out there who would pay good money for you to keep them entertained, and the little one here can entertain me."

Judy bent down as if to give me a kiss on the cheek, but instead hissed a whisper in my ear, "You be a good girl and do whatever Jake says." Then she disappeared into the crowd of people.

Jake patted the space next to him on the couch. I went over and sat down as far away from him as I could get. Jake motioned for me to move closer, but I was reluctant to do so. He grabbed my arm and pulled me over next to him. He lifted his arm around me, and the stench of sweat filled my nostrils and made me want to gag. His free hand started to rub gently on my leg, and I instinctively pulled them in close to me. He yanked them out straight again, his hand travelling further up my leg. Soon he was outside my panties, and I tried to push him away and get off the couch. He stood up, grabbing me by huge rough hands and lifted me against him. I frantically looked around for Judy, but she was nowhere in sight. Jake pushed open a door, walked into a bedroom and threw me on a disheveled bed.

Before I knew it, his big hands were beneath my dress, tearing at my panties. I tried to get away, but I was no match for him. He was laughing at my attempts, and I could feel his hot breath against my cheek. Suddenly, I felt a searing pain between my legs, and I let my mind travel to my secret place.

I have no idea how long I was in my secret place, or what all happened to me while I was there. I know that sunlight had been peeking through the tattered curtains when Jake threw me on the bed, and darkness was where the light had been. My panties were on the bed next to me, and I was so very sore between my legs. I put my hand down there and felt sticky moisture. There was blood on my hands when I grabbed my panties to put on. I lay motionless for a few minutes, wondering if I was going to be dead like Freckles. Then I slowly put my panties on and crept to the closed door.

I quietly cracked the door open. Music wasn't playing anymore. People were laying all over the floors and furniture, some of them partially dressed, and some of them totally naked, like Judy was. Snores and wheezes filled the air, and there was the distant growl of someone puking. I tiptoed over the bodies on the floor, stopping dead in my tracks if anyone moved.

I made it to the end of the couch where Jake and I had first been. My coat was flung across the end of it, resting on top of Judy's. I cautiously put it on, quiet as a little mouse. Then I grabbed Judy's coat, and made my way to the door. The front door opened quietly, and the cold night air blasted me in the face. I shivered, but wasn't sure if it was from the cold or fear. I made my way through the darkness to Cliff's parked car, opened the door, and crawled back to the back floorboard, covering myself with Judy's coat.

I was cold and the pangs of hunger attacked me, but I was more afraid of Jake finding me than the cold and hunger. I let Judy's coat hide me from the outside world, and once again escaped to my secret place.

The sun was breaking through the crystals of frost covering the car windows when I woke up. I had dreamed that I was in an ice castle, but a beautiful angel found me and wrapped her wings around me, melting the castle with the warmth of her love. I floated back to reality on feather wings, and when I opened my eyes, was disappointed to see where I was and shuttered remembering the events of the day before.

I heard my name being called in the distance, and hoped that the angel was coming to take me away again. Then I recognized Judy's frantic screaming of my name. I popped my head up to look out the window, and saw her coming towards the car. At the same instant she spotted me, and turned to yell to someone behind her, "It's Ok, I found her!"

Judy yanked open the car door, grabbed her coat off me, and once she had it on, took both my shoulders in her hands and shook me till I was dizzy asking, "What the hell's wrong with you? Why did you leave like that? They were turning the house upside down looking for you, and we sure as hell didn't need the cops showing up here. God, you're a pain in the ass!"

She threw me back in the car, went around to the driver's side and got in. Once she was on the road and had calmed down, she said, "Jake say's he really likes you."

"Well, I don't like him! He hurt me here," motioning between my legs as I said it. "I'm going to tell Daddy he hurt me."

With that, Judy hit me so hard that it slammed my head against the car door, and my chin and eye were cut open. Blood was gushing everywhere. Judy quickly pulled the car over, grabbed her scarf, and tried to stop the bleeding. Blood was running down the side of my face from my eye and pouring from the gash in my chin.

Judy frantically said, "You hold that on your chin tight. We're not far from the base and the infirmary. They'll take care of it there. You'll probably need to get sewed up."

Judy actually seemed concerned, and I was thinking that maybe she was really sorry for hitting me when she said, "If anyone asks—you fell off the jungle Jim at the park—you hear me?"

In too much pain and fear to say anything, I simply nodded. She was driving really fast, and I was bouncing all over the car. My head cracked against the car door a couple more times. She screeched to a halt when she reached the guardhouse at the entrance to the base, and quickly explained that she needed to get me to the infirmary. The guard quickly motioned for an escort car after she showed her ID card. The guard must have thought my throat had been cut, with all the blood.

When we reached the infirmary, the nurses rushed me back to a huge white room. A young doctor came in and in a soothing voice said, "Ok, honey, we're going to have put a couple of stitches in your chin. I'm going to give you a little shot that will take the pain away."

He no sooner got the words out of his mouth, than two nurses held me down on each side. I saw the needle coming towards my face, and squeezed my eyes shut tight. After a little stick and a burning sensation, the pain disappeared like the doctor said it would.

I don't know if I went to my special place, or was just floating along as a result of medication the doctor had given me, but when I woke up, I had three stitches right above my eyebrow, and six more in my chin, and hadn't felt a thing. As Judy was helping me out to the car, the doctor told me, "You need to be more careful on the playground--especially in this cold weather," giving Judy a suspicious look.

Judy and I didn't go into town for the next couple of days. The house was spotless when Cliff came home, and Judy was in a happy mood—thanks to whatever was in the bottle in the kitchen cabinet. Cliff made a big deal over my bandaged chin. When he asked how it happened, Judy quickly answered, "She fell off the Monkey bars on the playground." Then she gave me a look daring me to say anything different.

I longed to tell Cliff the truth, and to tell him how Jake had hurt me, but somehow I knew that if I revealed to anyone the pain I had suffered in the past, the future would be worse.

Judy and I did not go into town for the next few days. Judy said we had to get ready for our trip to see Nana. I was too excited to sleep for the week before we left. I kept going over in my mind all the exciting things to tell Nana—the bus rides, the sights and sounds of the big stores, the ice cream soda. I would tell her about my room and clothes and toys, only so she would know that Cliff was keeping his promise to take care of me. I knew I would have to lie about the cuts on my face, and I could never tell her about Jake and how he hurt me. Those were painful secrets that I would have to pack away with my other painful memories.

We left for Nana's on a Saturday at three o'clock in the morning. Cliff said it was to miss traffic, and I was half asleep when they loaded the car. I had a pillow and blanket in the back seat, so I slept most of the way there. I woke just as the sun was breaking the horizon, telling Judy and Cliff that I had to pee, and was hungry. We stopped at a truck stop and Judy and I went to the bathroom. Then we all sat down to a big breakfast. Cliff laughed and told Judy he couldn't believe that such a little girl could put away so much food.

Cliff said we were close to the farm, so I was too excited to go back to sleep. I watched the countryside zoom past me, anxious for the miles to disappear so I could see Nana again. Before long, we pulled into the barnyard. I think I was out of the car before it stopped, and ran to the familiar porch. The door swung open, and Nana welcomed me with open arms and a big smile. Right away, Nana asked me about the stitches in my chin and eye. It hurt me to lie to her, and I'm not sure she even believed me, because when I told her I hurt it at the park, she looked suspiciously at Judy.

The rooms of the old farm house had lost their familiarity. Boxes were piled up and the floors and walls were bare. I looked around, puzzled, and Nana said, "I sold the farm, Lizbeth. Everyone's going to help me move to town while you're here. You'll like the little house I'm moving to. It's close to the church, and I can walk just about anywhere I want to. And—no more farm chores!! Cliff was right; I'm getting too old to try to keep this place up."

I didn't want to put a damper on Nana's excitement, but I was disappointed not to be returning to the place that had provided me such security and love. Another good part of my life was being cut away and tossed aside like so much garbage. I grew sad at the thought of not visiting the farm again.

I soon learned that we weren't staying at the farm that night. We were all going to town and stay at the hotel. Nana had never stayed in a hotel before, and was very excited. I had no idea what a hotel was, but I figured it was a good thing. We grabbed a bag of Nana's and piled back in the car, Nana sitting in back with me. I scooted as close to Nana as I could possibly get.

It was a short drive to the outskirts of town, which was where the hotel was located. We had passed the hotel many times on our way to church, but thinking it just a big fancy house—I never gave it a second thought. You walked through a big porch to the counter where a woman talked to Cliff. Cliff said, "I would like two rooms for two nights please."

While Cliff was busy at the counter, Nana and I just wondered around the room that was furnished in big overstuffed chairs and couches, that were neither torn nor faded. There were lavish plants and flowers all around, and big ornate mirrors trimmed in gold. I thought for sure it must be the inside of a castle.

When Cliff was finished, the lady at the counter hit a little bell, and a young boy came out to get our bags. We a got into a closet, the door closed—and the closet moved. Everyone was laughing at the expression on my face! I had never seen such a thing before. It moved for a good two or three minutes, and when it stopped the young man said, "This is three," and the doors opened.

The man with our suitcases guided us down the hall and stopped at a door, which he unlocked and swung open. Judy said, "This is our room," showing the man which bags were hers and Cliff's. The young man then showed Nana and I to the room next door.

I ran over to the big window that was across from the door. From up high, the little backward town I had known looked more glamorous and refined. I felt pretty special to be in such a room, and Nana was just beside herself with excitement and curiosity. I told her what I knew about the black telephone that sat on the table, and then tried to explain the television. I had been fascinated by the television when I first went with Judy and Cliff. Cliff thought it was so cute when I tried to look inside the Television box to see where the people were, and wondering how I could get in there. It was something that was easier to show Nana than to try to explain, so I turned it on and we watched *I love Lucy,* which was one of my favorite shows.

Nana and I were laughing at the antics of *Lucy* when Judy came in. "I want you two to get your Sunday best on. We're all going to have lunch in the Hotel Dining room and I don't want you two looking like a couple of country bumpkins."

"What's a bumpkin?" I asked Nana. Nana smiled and said, "I guess it's what we are, Lizbeth. But your mother, her royal highness, forgets that she's one, too!"

Judy, with one hand on her hip and a smirk on face, said haughtily, "I just don't want you embarrassing Cliff. Nana, Cliff has something very important to talk to you about."

Nana and I met Cliff and Judy in the Hotel dining room about an hour later. Cliff stood up when we approached the table, held Nana's chair for her, and didn't sit down until all the females were seated. Then Cliff leaned across the table to me and said, "Lizbeth, we're going to be talking about something that you won't understand, but since it's about you and your future, I will try to explain it to you. Your Nana has custody of you-which means she has the say over what you can and can't do. I would like to adopt you—which means you carry my last name, and in the eyes of the courts, and the world, you are my daughter."

Nana and I had both been listening to Cliff intently. Cliff asked Nana, "Sadie, what do you think about the idea? I think of her as my daughter, and I love her as my daughter. If anything happens to me, I want to make sure she is treated *legally* as my daughter."

Nana nodded her head as Cliff spoke, and then turning to me, asked, "Lizbeth, what do you think? Are you happy being Cliff's little girl? And Cliff, what if you have children later on? Will you treat Lizbeth the same as them, or will you favor your natural child over her? This is a very serious step, and I hope you've studied on it long and hard, which is what I'm going to have to do."

"I didn't expect you to give me an answer right away. However, I think we both want what's best for Lizbeth. I couldn't love her anymore if she was my natural child, and if other children come along, I want her to feel part of the family by having the same last name. You think about it, you and Lizbeth talk about it, and let me know later on."

I sat on the sidelines during all this, nodding my head when Nana asked if I was happy. I didn't really understand what was going on. Wasn't I already Cliff's little girl? I called him Daddy, and although I wasn't sure about love—I know I was fond of him, and was beginning to trust him. Was I happy? I would be happy if Judy was not in my life—but then Cliff wouldn't be either. Why couldn't Judy be banished to some distant place, and I could just live with Cliff and Nana? My world would be perfect.

Nothing more was discussed about the 'adoption' during the rest of the meal. Nana's move became the main topic. She said that as we sat there eating, friends were picking up her stuff in their cars and trucks, and bringing it to her new house in town. "Don't you want to be at the farm for that?"Cliff asked.

"No." Nana said sadly. "I left the farm with you this morning on a happy note. If I'm there and watch them take stuff out of the house, I would probably break down and cry. That old farm has been my home for a long time, and there are a lot of memories there—good and bad. But, it's time to move on. I will, however, need to get to the new house before too long."

"We'll get finished here, and I will take you to the house. We can all help get it unloaded and put away—although you might not know where everything is." Cliff said light heartedly.

We finished lunch and Nana told Cliff we would meet him in the lobby, "Lizbeth and I need to get our workin' duds on!"

After changing clothes, we went down to the lobby and then over to Nana's house. It was a small house, on a corner lot on the west side of town. It was a poor section of town, but Nana's house was one of the nicest, and a lot nicer than the farmhouse. She had a good sized yard that she said would be beautiful once she got her flowers planted in the spring, and had plenty of room for a vegetable garden.

Friends in trucks were already at Nana's when we got there. They were all standing around visiting with each other, patiently awaiting Nana's arrival. When we pulled up, it was like the start of a party. There was a sense of festivity in the air as people lifted and moved boxes and pieces of furniture, asking Nana where to put this or that. I was trying to help, but began to think I was in the way more than helping.

It didn't take long for the last of Nana's possessions to be brought from the farm. When Mrs. Johnson's husband pulled up and said he had the last load, a group cheer went up. Cliff found me and said, "Let's go get some sandwiches for the troops, Lizbeth. Think you could help me with that?"

Cliff and I left to go to the fast food drive-in about a block away. When we got back, Cliff made me feel important by putting me in charge of handing out hamburgers. Everyone had gathered inside Nana's little house, sitting and standing wherever they could find a spot. Nana thanked everyone for helping her move, and then they started leaving one by one. Nana looked very happy—and sad.

Everything was in great disarray in the little house, but Nana said she wasn't worried about it. "I got over forty years of memories crammed into this house in one day. I'm not about to get it all straightened out and organized in another. I will simply take it one day at a time, and savor each memory as it's unpacked and comes to rest in the proper place."

That night, as Nana and I lay in the hotel room, Nana said, "Lizbeth, Cliff is a good man. I feel confident that he's going to be a good daddy to you, and I have to think about what would happen to you if something happened to me. I think Cliff has even made your mama a better woman. How her foul temperament ever attracted a man like Cliff is beyond me. She seems to have settled down, and she really loves Cliff, I think. You're with them anyway, so you might as well be 'Lizbeth Sweeney' and have a chance at a normal family life. I know he can give you a much better life than I ever could, and you deserve that. I want you to know that I would sign those adoption papers only because I love you so much, and want what's best for you. Lizbeth, you are happy with Cliff and Judy, aren't you?"

I lay there in the dark, pondering the same questions I had asked myself at lunch. I would be happy if Judy wasn't in my life, but since she was, I had no choice but to endure whatever came my way. Maybe Judy would change with time, and she might even grow to like me. I knew I could never let anyone know the unhappiness and pain I found at her hand, so there was nothing to do but continue on, hoping that things would get better. I answered Nana as best I could without lying, "Yes, Nana. Daddy is very good to me, and I'm happy living with him."

The next morning we all went to Church together. Afterwards, we took Nana back to the farm to pick up the old truck and give her a chance to have a look around, making sure she got everything. Tears welled up as she took a last look around. I rode back to town with Nana, and by the time we met up with Cliff and Judy, they had our bags loaded in the car. We would be heading back to our home that afternoon. However, we were all going to have lunch at the local diner before we did.

Over lunch, Nana told Cliff that she would sign the adoption papers. Cliff and Judy were happy with the announcement. On the way to the car Cliff said, "Sadie, I've arranged for a telephone to be installed at your place. That way you can talk to Lizbeth anytime you feel the need."

Nana was touched but said, "I appreciate the gesture, but I really can't afford the expense"

"I will be responsible for the bill. It's my gift to you, Sadie," Cliff told Nana. Tears welled up in Nana's eyes and she gave Cliff a big hug. We took Nana back home, where we said our goodbyes, and headed back to our own home.

It was dark when we reached our house, and I was half asleep as Cliff carried me in, pulled off my coat and shoes, and tucked me into bed. He brushed my hair back from my face, gave me a kiss on the forehead and said, "I love you, Lizbeth. By the end of next month, you will really be my little girl."

In the next few days, Judy and I decorated the house and tree for Christmas. I was happy that we didn't go to the city, although I missed the bus rides, but it was fun getting everything ready for the holiday. Judy and I baked cookies, and during this time, I almost thought Judy was starting to show some mothering tendencies I never knew she had. She laughed when I got icing everywhere while decorating cookies, and didn't lose her temper once. Maybe this 'adoption' thing was really a good thing, and caused Judy to look at me differently.

Two days before Christmas, Cliff and Judy were going to a Christmas party at the Club on base. They both got all dressed up, and Judy looked beautiful in her red party dress, with her raven hair flowing down her back. Cliff was dressed in his blue uniform, and he looked so handsome to me. One of the neighbor teenagers came to stay with me while they were gone to the party. Her name was Mandy, and we had hot chocolate and Christmas cookies, and watched television. Cliff had said I could stay up till they came home, but as hard as I tried to stay awake, I finally lost the battle around midnight and fell asleep on the couch.

Loud voices coming from the kitchen woke me. Mandy was gone, and it didn't take me long to realize that Judy and Cliff were not happy with each other. I heard Cliff say loudly, "I'm just saying that you can't go to these functions and get so damn drunk that you lose control. You're suppose to pace yourself, and conduct yourself like a lady with some sophistication. I work with these people, and I don't want them thinking you're some kind of a tramp or something. Your actions tonight were an embarrassment!"

Judy's words were slurred as she yelled back, "Screw those goody two shoes if they can't loosen up a little. I was just dancing. The guys didn't seem to mind. You're too much of a prude to really have a good time!"

"You're drunk, and I'm not going to continue this discussion. We'll talk about it when you're sober, if there ever is such a time!" Cliff shot back to Judy on his way into the living room.

I pretended to be asleep, and Cliff came over to the couch and covered me with a blanket. Judy had followed him into the room, but when she started to say something, Cliff said quietly, "Keep your voice down. You'll wake Lizbeth."

Cliff and Judy disappeared into their room, and I didn't hear anymore that night. The next day there was a tension between them, but they tried to pretend that everything was normal. I left cookies and milk out for Santa before going to bed, and tried hard to stay awake to see Santa, but I just couldn't do it.

Christmas morning I awoke and rushed to the living room to find packages and toys heaped beneath the tree. I got everything I had ever dreamed of and even more. I was so excited, and after breakfast we called Nana to wish her a Merry Christmas, and I told her of all the wonderful presents I had gotten. I longed to be with her, but hearing her voice and sharing my excitement with her would have to do. Nana said, "I'm glad Santa was so good to you. This year will soon be over, and the new one promises to be bright. It will hold good things for you, Lizbeth."

I hung up the telephone after talking to Nana, hoping she was right about the coming year, but couldn't help feeling a little blue. So many changes had taken place in my life and how many more where to come?

The New Year brought snow—and a lot of it. I would don my boots, mittens and hat and head outside and the little girl next door, Becky, and I would build snowmen and forts until tiny crystals of ice hung from our noses and eyelashes. We would go in only long enough to warm up, and then we were at it again.

One evening, Daddy brought home a sled. After dinner, he took me to a neighborhood hill, and he showed me how to use it. I couldn't remember having so much fun, riding down the snow glistened hill, the stars starting to peek out in the sky overhead. The night air and the coldness soon wore us both out, and we started home. I went to sleep that night eagerly, wanting the morning to come quickly so I could show Becky my sled.

Judy was getting very cranky and would snap at me often. I always did my chores, hoping to give her no cause to get upset with me, but no matter how hard I tried to do everything perfectly, it was never good enough. I was always glad to escape to the outdoors, no matter how cold or severe the weather was. Often times I would come in and Judy would be asleep on the couch, a bottle always within reach. It would be up to me to get my own lunch, and would often start peeling potatoes for dinner before she woke up.

It seemed that with each passing day I was taking over more and more of her responsibilities. I had learned to do the laundry, and if I stood on a chair to reach the stove, I could do a lot of the cooking. Daddy and Judy were arguing a lot now about Judy's 'drinking.'

In early March Daddy came home with an official looking piece of paper. He said that the adoption was final, and the piece of paper was my birth certificate showing that my legal name was 'Lizbeth Sweeney' and that I was officially his little girl. He seemed very happy about it all, so I was happy too, even though I didn't really understand it all. Judy didn't show any emotion one way or the other, just sat at the table, puffing on her cigarette and looking bored. She told Daddy, "If I don't get out of this house soon—I'm going to lose my mind!"

"The weather is starting to clear off, so you should be able to go out in a couple of days. What did you have in mind?" Daddy asked Judy.

"I thought I'd take Lizbeth to a movie or something. Anything to be out of the house," was Judy's reply.

"If you want to, you can take me to work in the morning and keep the car and go do something. Just pick me up at five," Daddy said to Judy.

Judy seemed to like that idea and was in a cheerful mood the rest of the evening. The next morning, she was up and dressed, and rushed me to get ready in time to take Daddy to work. We dropped him off on base, and then we headed to town. Daddy had suggested going to the movie on base, but Judy said they weren't showing anything she wanted to see. She said we would do some window shopping, have an early lunch and then catch a matinee. She told Daddy we would be out in plenty of time to pick him up at five.

The drive into town nearly scared me to death. The roads were still slushy with snow, and Judy was driving fast. Sometimes the car would slip and slide, and a couple of times we almost slid into other cars. Judy would laugh when that happened, and then ask, "Wasn't that fun?" when the near collisions were past. I just held my breath and kept my eyes tightly clenched, thinking it would be different if Daddy was driving, because he was always careful. I was happy when Judy finally parked the car in a lot close to the movie theater.

We first stopped at a little drug store. Judy had me sit on a seat at the soda counter, ordered me an ice cream soda, and then left to go to the pay phone in front of the drug store. I had my soda nearly finished when she finally came back. She sat down next to me and ordered a cup of coffee. She kept looking at her watch while drinking her coffee, and then finally said, "Let's go. I'm meeting a friend at the restaurant for lunch. I want you to be on your best behavior, okay?"

I climbed off the stool, put my coat on and followed her out the door. We walked a block to a little diner, and once inside, she waved to a soldier sitting in one of the back booths, and we quickly made our way to him. It was a soldier I had never seen before, but Judy called him 'Jimmy' and gave him a hug and kiss when she saw him.

Judy sat next to the soldier in the booth, and I sat across from both of them. Judy ordered a hamburger for both of us, but she only ate a couple of bites of hers. She was too busy giving Jimmy all her attention and I couldn't help but imagine how angry Daddy would be if he was to see the way she was carrying on. I was just a kid, but I knew enough to be embarrassed by their actions. I couldn't eat much of my hamburger, partly because the soda had filled me up, and partly because the way they were acting made me a little queasy.

After a while Judy said to the soldier, "Why don't we get Lizbeth settled in the movie, and then we can take care of business?" giving Jimmy a wink as she said it. Jimmy was eager to oblige, and quickly paid the cashier for our food, and the three of us left together for the short walk to the theater.

Peter Pan was the movie that was playing, and I was excited about seeing it. Judy told the lady at the ticket counter that she only wanted one ticket, but would like to go in with me to get me some popcorn and get me settled. When I asked Judy, "Aren't you going to see the movie too?" she quickly said. "No, I have some errands to run. I'll be back to get you when the movie is over, so wait for me right here."

Judy took me inside, bought a big tub of popcorn and a coke for me, and she and the usher saw me to my seat. Then Judy left. Judy's leaving didn't bother me at all after the theater darkened and the movie started. I was lost in *Never-Never Land* with *Peter Pan*, and the rest of the world was a thousand miles away.

I hated to see the movie end, forcing me back to reality, but I waited until most of the people left before leaving my seat and heading for the entrance. The lady who had been taking tickets asked where my parents were, and I replied, "My mama will pick me up in a little while." She told me I could wait by the big glass door on the inside, because it was a little cold.

I waited, and waited and waited—but no Judy. The ticket lady asked if she could call someone, but I shook my head no, reassuring her that my mother was coming. She apologized, and told me I would have to wait outside, because they were closing the theater for awhile. I stepped out into the cold.

Again I waited and waited. The afternoon sun was sinking into night, and I was beginning to get scared. Several people stopped and asked if I was lost, and I would say I was waiting for my mother. The cold air was seeping through my coat, and my nose and ears were numb.

A policeman had just stopped by me and started asking questions when Judy pulled up in the car. She jumped out and explained to the policeman she had gone to get the car. The policeman looked at her suspiciously and asked, "Where was your car parked, Lady? We got calls on this little girl standing out here for a couple of hours."

Judy looked innocent as she replied, "There must be some mistake, officer. I've only been gone a few minutes."

Then Judy hustled me into the car, got in herself, and we took off for home. "It's almost 6:00 and Daddy is going to be pissed because we're late. We're going to tell him we had car trouble," she said, looking at me angrily. "We had car trouble. Do you understand?"

If the ride to town was scary, the ride home was terrifying. Judy was driving very, very fast and almost lost control on a couple of turns. I was too tired and cold to show any emotion, but on the inside I was praying we would be home soon, and yet dreading our arrival because I knew there was going to be a fight.

Judy went on base and stopped by Daddy's work, but one of the guys told her Daddy had waited for awhile, and then got a ride home from one of the other guys. Judy sped off towards home.

Daddy was usually pretty agreeable, and he didn't get angry too often, but Judy was the one person who get make him lose his temper. I knew this was going to be one of those times, and I was right. When we pulled into the driveway, Daddy was out the front door in an instant. "Where the hell have you been?" he asked Judy angrily. "I've been worried sick!"

"I couldn't get the car started!" Judy shot back defensively. "I don't know if I left the lights on or what, but the battery was dead. I tried and tried to start it, and finally a nice man gave me a jump start." Then Judy began to cry. "I'm sorry you worried. I just didn't know what to do!'

Daddy put his arms around Judy. "I'm sorry I snapped at you. I was just so worried. Come on, don't cry."

I was glad that Daddy didn't ask me about the car 'problem' because I hated to lie to him, but knew Judy would inflict pain if I didn't back up her story. But Daddy seemed satisfied with Judy's explanation, and we went in the house and got dinner ready.

Over dinner, Daddy said 'uncle Sam' was going to send him out of town again, and he would be gone a week to ten days. "This business with the car worries me though," Daddy said to Judy. "I'm giving you the number of a mechanic. He has a tow truck, so if you're out and have problems again, you give him a call right away."

Judy spent the rest of the evening getting Daddy's bags packed for his trip. The next morning we ate breakfast and then drove Daddy to the airfield on base. We watched him get on the plane, and watched the plane take off. I loved watching the big machines start down the runway and then soar off into the sky. We stayed for awhile, watching the planes landing and taking off. Then we went to the Commissary to buy some groceries.

When we got home, Judy told me to put the groceries away, which I started doing right away. Judy made a telephone call, and she was on the phone the whole time I was putting the groceries away and doing the breakfast dishes. I busied myself with the rest of the household chores, and when I was finished with them, Judy was still on the phone. She had her legs thrown over the arm of the sofa and was talking and smoking, occasionally giggling like a schoolgirl. I interrupted long enough to ask if I could go outside to play, but she just motioned me away with the wave of her hand, so I took that as a yes.

My friend Becky and I played outside most of the day, stopping long enough to ask if I could eat lunch at Becky's house. Judy was still talking on the phone, and once again waved me away, so I ate lunch with Becky.

It was nice to be in a home where the mother was actually a

mother. She fixed the sandwiches, served them to us, and cleaned up afterwards. I asked if she wanted me to help, but she said I didn't have to do anything but wash my hands and be a little girl. I asked Becky if she had to do chores, and she said she took out the trash and picked up her toys, and that was about it. I envied Becky, and wished my mother and hers could trade places. But then, I wouldn't want Becky to know what my mother was like, because I wouldn't wish Judy on anyone. Nana's words came back to haunt me, "Judy is my cross to bear."

Becky and I played into the late afternoon on her swing. Becky's mom had just come out to tell her that she had to come in to get ready for dinner, when we all noticed a car pull into my driveway. Three men and two women got out of the car, and each man was carrying a case of beer. My heart sunk as I recognized Jake. My fear must have shown on my face, because Becky asked if I wanted her to ask Judy if I could spend the night with Becky. I was afraid Judy would be drunk by now, because she had been drinking all day, and I knew how ugly she could be when she was drunk. I would be embarrassed to have Becky and her mom see Judy like that, so I slowly shook my head no and went home with a heavy, fearful heart.

I went in the house and right away Jake says, "There's my little angel. I was afraid I wouldn't get to see you!" He came over to me and tried to pick me up, but I squirmed out of his grip.

"Lizbeth, you say hello to everyone! I won't tolerate you being rude!" Judy said, slurring every word.

"Hello," I said softly, and then asked Judy, "Is dinner ready?"

"I'm busy right now, Lizbeth. You can fix yourself something, can't you?" was her reply.

I made my way to the kitchen, and fixed a bowl of cereal. I could feel Jake's eyes on me the whole time and I was so uncomfortable that I couldn't finish the bowl of cereal. I finally gave up and went to my room, closing the door behind me, trying to block the loud music, laughter and voices coming from the living room. I put my nightgown on and climbed into bed, taking a couple of my favorite toys with me. One of those toys was *View-Master* that Daddy had given to me. I loved to look through it and see far-away places. This was a night for escape, so I lost myself in the 3-D world.

I must have fallen asleep looking at the scenes through the *View-Master*, but sometime later I awoke with hot, smelly beer-breath in my face. I saw Jake leering down at me, and sat up with a start. He had pulled the blankets back, and his huge rough hand was sliding up the inside of my thigh. I started kicking, and I must have kicked him in the groin, because he hauled off and hit me on the side of my face with his fist. I fell back on the bed in shock and pain. He pulled my legs apart and his hands started exploring my body. I started to scream, but the noise from the other room drowned out my screams, or they just went unnoticed.

Jake kept telling me to 'shut up' and pulled my panties off and stuffed them in my mouth. I clinched my eyes shut tight, and in between my gasping for breath and tears of pain, I left that place and went to another—one where there was no pain and fear.

I awoke the next morning. My face was sore, and my body was bruised and aching. There was blood on my nightgown and sheets. I went into the bathroom, pulled up my footstool, and looked in the mirror. My cheek was black and blue, and my eye was bloodshot. I pulled off my nightgown, and noticed bruises on the inside of my thighs. I went to use the bathroom, but it burned when I peed. My head was pounding so hard, I thought it would explode. I forced myself to get dressed, wincing in pain with every movement.

I went into the living room and found Judy sprawled out on the couch, half dressed. Beer bottles were thrown everywhere, and the ashtrays were over flowing. Judy didn't move, even when I started clearing away the mess. I was half hoping she was dead, but when I got close enough, noticed her low snore. She was still alive. I wasn't sure if I was happy about that or not.

I was almost finished cleaning up when there was a soft knock at the door. It was Becky. She looked shocked when she saw me. "What happened to your face?" she asked.

"I fell out of bed and hit the table," I replied. I knew she wouldn't understand if I told her what really happened. I wasn't sure I did. She asked if I wanted to come out to play, but I told her I wasn't feeling too good, which was the truth.

Judy never asked about my face, and I never bothered to tell her, knowing it would have done no good. I just kept to myself for the next few days, eagerly looking forward to Daddy's return.

Daddy was not happy when he got home. Most of the people who lived in our neighborhood worked with Daddy on the base, including Becky's Daddy and the story about Judy's loud party was all over the base when he returned. He confronted Judy with the story, and she admitted she had had a party saying, "Those damn busy bodies should mind their own damn business!"

"I told you to watch your behavior. Military families are close knit, just like a small town. Your behavior reflects back on me, and could end up ruining my career. If you want to act like a whore, fine—we'll get a divorce and you can be a whore!" Daddy yelled at Judy. "Another thing—did you hit Lizbeth in one of your drunken fits and leave that bruise on her face?"

I didn't think Daddy would notice the bruise because it had faded quite a bit, but he had. I quickly told him the story about falling out of bed, hoping to bring peace to the situation.

Daddy finally asked Judy, "Well, Judy, what's it going to be? Are you going to settle down and conduct yourself like a proper wife, or do we get a divorce?"

Judy looked at Daddy, tears welling up in her eyes and said, "I'm sorry I had the party. I just get so lonely when you're not around. I'll try to be a better wife. I don't want a divorce. I'm pregnant."

Late January brought snow—and a lot of it. I would don my boots and mittens and hat and head outside and the little girl next door, Becky, and I would build snowmen and forts until tiny crystals of ice hung from our noses and eyelashes. We would go in only long enough to warm up, and then we were at it again.

Judy was getting very cranky and would snap at me often. I always did my chores, hoping to give her no cause to get upset with me, but no matter how hard I tried to do everything perfectly, it was never good enough. I was always glad to escape to the outdoors, no matter how cold or severe the weather was. Often times I would come in and Judy would be asleep on the couch, a bottle always within reach. It would be up to me to get my own lunch, and would often start peeling potatoes for dinner before she woke up.

It seemed that with each passing day I was taking over more and more of her responsibilities. I had learned to do the laundry, and if I stood on a chair to reach the stove, I could do a lot of the cooking. Daddy and Judy were arguing a lot now about Judy's 'drinking.'

In early March Daddy came home with an official looking piece of paper. He said that the adoption was final, and the piece of paper was my birth certificate showing that my legal name was 'Lizbeth Sweeney' and that I was officially his little girl. He seemed very happy about it all, so I was happy too, even though I didn't really understand it all. Judy didn't show any emotion one way or the other, just sat at the table, puffing on her cigarette and looking bored. She told Daddy, "If I don't get out of this house soon—I'm going to lose my mind!"

"The weather is starting to clear off, so you should be able to go out in a couple of days. What did you have in mind?" Daddy asked Judy.

"I thought I'd take Lizbeth to a movie or something. Anything to be out of the house," was Judy's reply.

"If you want to, you can take me to work in the morning and keep the car and go do something. Just pick me up at five," Daddy said to Judy.

Judy seemed to like that idea and was in a cheerful mood the rest of the evening. The next morning, she was up and dressed, and rushed me to get ready in time to take Daddy to work. We dropped him off on base, and then we headed to town. Daddy had suggested going to the movie on base, but Judy said they weren't showing anything she wanted to see. She said we would do some window shopping, have an early lunch and then catch a matinee. She told Daddy we would be out in plenty of time to pick him up at five.

The drive into town nearly scared me to death. The roads were still slushy with snow, and Judy was driving fast. Sometimes the car would slip and slide, and a couple of times we almost slid into other cars. Judy would laugh when that happened, and then ask, "Wasn't that fun?" when the near collisions were past. I just held my breath and kept my eyes tightly clenched, thinking it would be different if Daddy was driving, because he was always careful. I was happy when Judy finally parked the car in a lot close to the movie theater.

We first stopped at a little drug store. Judy had me sit on a seat at the soda counter, ordered me an ice cream soda, and then left to go to the pay phone in front of the drug store. I had my soda nearly finished when she finally came back. She sat down next to me and ordered a cup of coffee. She kept looking at her watch while drinking her coffee, and then finally said, "Let's go. I'm meeting a friend at the restaurant for lunch. I want you to be on your best behavior, okay?"

I climbed off the stool, put my coat on and followed her out the door. We walked a block to a little diner, and once inside, she waved to a soldier sitting in one of the back booths, and we quickly made our way him. It was a soldier I had never seen before, but Judy called him 'Jimmy' and gave him a hug and kiss when she saw him.

Judy sat next to the soldier in the booth, and I sat across from both of them. Judy ordered a hamburger for both of us, but she only ate a couple of bites of hers. She was too busy giving Jimmy all her attention and I couldn't help but imagine how angry Daddy would be if he was to see the way she was carrying on. I was only five years old, but I knew enough to be embarrassed by their actions. I couldn't eat much of my hamburger, partly because the soda had filled me up, and partly because the way they were acting made me a little queasy.

After a while Judy said to the soldier, "Why don't we get Lizbeth settled in the movie, and then we can take care of business?" giving Jimmy a wink as she said it. Jimmy was eager to oblige, and quickly paid the cashier for our food, and the three of us left together for the short walk to the theater.

Peter Pan was the movie that was playing, and I was excited about seeing it. Judy told the lady at the ticket counter that she only wanted one ticket, but would like to go in with me to get me some popcorn and get me settled. When I asked Judy, "Aren't you going to see the movie too?" she quickly said. "No, I have some errands to run. I'll be back to get you when the movie is over, so wait for me right here."

Judy took me inside, bought a big tub of popcorn and a coke for me, and she and the usher saw me to my seat. Then Judy left. Judy's leaving didn't bother me at all after the theater darkened and the movie started. I was lost in *Never-Never Land* with *Peter Pan*, and the rest of the world was a thousand miles away.

I hated to see the movie end, forcing me back to reality, but I waited until most of the people left before leaving my seat and heading for the entrance. The lady who had been taking tickets asked where my parents were, and I replied, "My mama will pick me up in a little while." She told me I could wait by the big glass door on the inside, because it was a little cold.

I waited, and waited and waited—but no Judy. The ticket lady asked if she could call someone, but I shook my head no, reassuring her that my mother was coming. She apologized, and told me I would have to wait outside, because they were closing the theater for awhile. I stepped out into the cold.

Again I waited and waited. The afternoon sun was sinking into night, and I was beginning to get scared. Several people stopped and asked if I was lost, and I would say I was waiting for my mother. The cold air was seeping through my coat, and my nose and ears were numb.

A policeman had just stopped by me and started asking questions when Judy pulled up in the car. She jumped out and explained to the policeman she had gone to get the car. The policeman looked at her suspiciously and asked, "Where was your car parked, Lady? We got calls on this little girl standing out here for hours."

Judy looked innocent as she replied, "There must be some mistake, officer. I've only been gone a few minutes."

Then Judy hustled me into the car, got in herself, and we took off for home. "It's almost 6:00 and Daddy is going to be pissed because we're late. We're going to tell him we had car trouble," she said, looking at me angrily. "We had car trouble. Do you understand?"

If the ride to town was scary, the ride home was terrifying. Judy was driving very, very fast and almost lost control on a couple of turns. I was too tired and cold to show any emotion, but on the inside I was praying we would be home soon, and yet dreading our arrival because I knew there was going to be a fight.

Judy went on base and stopped by Daddy's work, but one of the guys told her Daddy had waited for awhile, and then got a ride home from one of the other guys. Judy sped off towards home.

Daddy was usually pretty agreeable, and he didn't get angry too often, but Judy was the one person who could make him lose his temper. I knew this was going to be one of those times, and I was right. When we pulled into the driveway, Daddy was out the front door in an instant. "Where the hell have you been?" he asked Judy angrily. "I've been worried sick!"

"I couldn't get the car started!" Judy shot back defensively. "I don't know if I left the lights on or what, but the battery was dead. I tried and tried to start it, and finally a nice man gave me a jump start."Then

Judy began to cry. "I'm sorry you worried. I just didn't know what to do!'

Daddy put his arms around Judy. "I'm sorry I snapped at you. I was just so worried. Come on, don't cry."

I was glad that Daddy didn't ask me about the car 'problem' because I hated to lie to him, but knew Judy would inflict pain if I didn't back up her story. But Daddy seemed satisfied with Judy's explanation, and we went in the house and got dinner ready.

Over dinner, Daddy said 'uncle Sam' was going to send him out of town again, and he would be gone a week to ten days. "This business with the car worries me though," Daddy said to Judy. "I'm giving you the number of a mechanic. He has a tow truck, so if you're out and have problems again, you give him a call right away."

Judy spent the rest of the evening getting Daddy's bags packed for his trip. The next morning we ate breakfast and then drove Daddy to the airfield on base. We watched him get on the plane, and watched the plane take off. I loved watching the big machines start down the runway and then soar off into the sky. We stayed for awhile, watching the planes landing and taking off. Then we went to the Commissary to buy some groceries.

When we got home, Judy told me to put the groceries away, which I started doing right away. Judy made a telephone call, and she was on the phone the whole time I was putting the groceries away and doing the breakfast dishes. I busied myself with the rest of the household chores, and when I was finished with them, Judy was still on the phone. She had her legs thrown over the arm of the sofa and was talking and smoking, occasionally giggling like a schoolgirl. I interrupted long enough to ask if I could go outside to play, but she just motioned me away with the wave of her hand, so I took that as a yes.

My friend Becky and I played outside most of the day, stopping long enough to ask if I could eat lunch at Becky's house. Judy was still talking on the phone, and once again waved me away, so I ate lunch with Becky.

It was nice to be in a home where the mother was actually a mother. She fixed the sandwiches, served them to us, and cleaned up afterwards. I asked if she wanted me to help, but she said I didn't have to do anything but wash my hands and be a little girl. I asked Becky if she had to do chores, and she said she took out the trash and picked up her toys, and that was about it. I envied Becky, and wished my mother and hers could trade places. But then, I wouldn't want Becky to know what my mother was like, because I wouldn't wish Judy on anyone. Nana's words came back to haunt me, "Judy was my cross to bear."

Becky and I played into the late afternoon on her swing. Becky's mom had just come out to tell her that she had to come in to get ready for dinner, when we all noticed a car pull into my driveway. Three men and two women got out of the car, and each man was carrying a case of beer. My heart sunk as I recognized Jake. My fear must have shown on my face, because Becky asked if I wanted her to ask Judy if I could spend the night with Becky. I was afraid Judy would be drunk by now, because she had been drinking all day, and I knew how ugly she could be when she was drunk. I would be embarrassed to have Becky and her mom see Judy like that, so I slowly shook my head no and went home with a heavy, fearful heart.

I went in the house and right away Jake says, "There's my little angel. I was afraid I wouldn't get to see you!" He came over to me and tried to pick me up, but I squirmed out of his grip.

"Lizbeth, you say hello to everyone! I won't tolerate you being rude!" Judy said, slurring every word.

"Hello," I said softly, and then asked Judy, "Is dinner ready?"

"I'm busy right now, Lizbeth. You can fix yourself something, can't you?" was her reply.

I made my way to the kitchen, and fixed a bowl of cereal. I could feel Jake's eyes on me the whole time and I was so uncomfortable that I couldn't finish the bowl of cereal. I finally gave up and went to my room, closing the door behind me, trying to block the loud music, laughter and voices coming from the living room. I put my nightgown on and climbed into bed, taking a couple of my favorite toys with me. One of those toys was *View-Master* that Daddy had given to me. I loved to look through it and see far-away places. This was a night for escape, so I lost myself in the 3-D world.

I must have fallen asleep looking at the scenes through the *View-Master*, but sometime later I awoke with hot, smelly beer-breath in my face. I saw Jake leering down at me, and sat up with a start. He had pulled the blankets back, and his huge rough hand was sliding up the inside of my thigh. I started kicking, and I must have kicked him in the groin, because he hauled off and hit me on the side of my face with his fist. I fell back on the bed in shock and pain. He pulled my legs apart and his hands started exploring my body. I started to scream, but the noise from the other room drowned out my screams, or they just went unnoticed.

Jake kept telling me to 'shut up' and pulled my panties off and stuffed them in my mouth. I clinched my eyes shut tight, and in between my gasping for breath and tears of pain, I left that place and went to another—one where there was no pain and fear.

I awoke the next morning. My face was sore, and my body was bruised and aching. There was blood on my nightgown and sheets. I went into the bathroom, pulled up my footstool, and looked in the mirror. My cheek was black and blue, and my eye was bloodshot. I pulled off my nightgown, and noticed bruises on the inside of my thighs. I went to use the bathroom, but it burned when I peed. My head was pounding so hard, I thought it would explode. I forced myself to get dressed, wincing in pain with every movement.

I went into the living room and found Judy sprawled out on the couch, half dressed. Beer bottles were thrown everywhere, and the ashtrays were over flowing. Judy didn't move, even when I started clearing away the mess. I was half hoping she was dead, but when I got close enough, noticed her low snore. She was still alive. I wasn't sure if I was happy about that or not.

I was almost finished cleaning up when there was a soft knock at the door. It was Becky. She looked shocked when she saw me. "What happened to your face?" she asked.

"I fell out of bed and hit the table," I replied. I knew she wouldn't understand if I told her what really happened. I wasn't sure I did. She asked if I wanted to come out to play, but I told her I wasn't feeling too good, which was the truth.

Judy never asked about my face, and I never bothered to tell her, knowing it would have done no good. I just kept to myself for the next few days, eagerly looking forward to Daddy's return.

Daddy was not happy when he got home. Most of the people who lived in our neighborhood worked with Daddy on the base, including Becky's Daddy and the story about Judy's loud party was all over the base when he returned. He confronted Judy with the story, and she admitted she had had a party saying, "Those damn busy bodies should mind their own damn business!"

"I told you to watch your behavior. Military families are close knit, just like a small town. Your behavior reflects back on me, and could end up ruining my career. If you want to act like a whore, fine—we'll get a divorce and you can be a whore!" Daddy yelled at Judy. "Another thing—did you hit Lizbeth in one of your drunken fits and leave that bruise on her face?"

I didn't think Daddy would notice the bruise because it had faded quite a bit, but he had. I quickly told him the story about falling out of bed, hoping to bring peace to the situation.

Daddy finally asked Judy, "Well, Judy, what's it going to be? Are you going to settle down and conduct yourself like a proper wife, or do we get a divorce?"

Judy looked at Daddy, tears welling up in her eyes and said, "I'm sorry I had the party. I just get so lonely when you're not around. I'll try to be a better wife. I don't want a divorce. I'm pregnant."

The announcement that Judy was pregnant came as a surprise to everyone, and as soon as Daddy explained what that meant, I was beside myself with joy. I was going to have a baby brother or sister. The only disappointment was the fact that it would take so long for the baby to arrive.

In just a short time, the baby was responsible for changes that affected my life. Judy was too sick to drink beer, smoke cigarettes, or to go to parties. All she did was throw up and sleep. Of course, I was the one to try to keep the house in some sort of order, and I enjoyed helping Daddy fix the evening meal. Judy said the sight and smell of food cooking made her ill. But, she was able to eat, even if she didn't keep it all down.

Daddy and I did all the shopping for the nursery on his days off. We couldn't wait to get the crib together, and while most of the tiny clothes we bought were white, yellow or green, I was intrigued with the smallness of them. Daddy said once the baby was born, then we could by frilly pink dresses or rough and tough blue outfits. We added bottles and diapers and bibs to the supply, and while I think Daddy was hoping for a little boy, I was praying for a little girl.

The days turned into months and Judy's stomach got bigger and bigger. She couldn't get out of the overstuffed chair without help, and she was even too sick to be grouchy. She said more than once that being pregnant was 'hell,' but it was pure heaven to me. It was a lot of work for a little girl, but I didn't mind, because I hadn't been hit or kicked or had my hair pulled since Judy started getting sick.

The baby was due in about 4 months when I got sick. I was running a high fever and was achy and throwing up. The fever was very high one night, so high that Daddy bundled me up in a blanket and rushed me to the base hospital. They couldn't get my fever down, so they kept me. Daddy stayed at the hospital the whole night, sleeping in a chair next to my bed. He told me later that I was talking out of my head about spiders and monsters and someone named Jake.

The next day, a rash came out on my face, and as the day progressed, it moved further down my body. I heard the doctor tell Daddy that I had *German measles*, and that if my mother was pregnant, she needed to see the doctor right away, because it could cause a miscarriage. I didn't know what that meant, but from the tone the doctor used, and the look on Daddy's face—I knew it wasn't a good thing.

"Is Judy going to die?" I later asked Daddy. The thought didn't upset me, except I was concerned for my baby brother or sister.

"Of course not!" Daddy replied. "Why would you think such a thing?"

"'Cause of the 'carriage' thing the doctor said," I said as tears welled.

"Don't you worry, sweetheart! Everything is fine. The doctor just meant he would have to keep an eye on your mother." His words calmed my fears and eased my concerns for the baby.

I was able to go home in about a week, but the doctors continued to keep a close eye on Judy for awhile. Finally they said they didn't think there was any danger to the baby, because Judy never got the measles. The doctors may have said the baby was out of danger, but I still said a prayer every night for God and the angels to watch over my baby brother or sister.

A few months later, Daddy woke me up in the middle of the night to say we had to go to the hospital. I put my coat on over my nightgown, and hurriedly pulled on my shoes and socks. Daddy helped Judy to the car, who was holding her stomach and declaring she was going to die, but in the same breath stated how happy she would be to "have this kid out of me!"

Daddy and I waited in the waiting room for what seemed like hours. Finally the doctor came out and told Daddy it was over, "Baby and mother are fine. It's a beautiful baby girl."

I was so excited that I jumped up and down, and Daddy had to remind me that we were in a hospital, so I had to be quiet. We went to the nursery, and I got to see my baby sister for the first time. She was so tiny and fragile looking with a mop of brown hair and long curly eyelashes. I couldn't see her eyes, because she was sound asleep, but I was sure they were beautiful. She was a perfect little baby doll, and I couldn't wait till we could bring her home.

It was three or four days before Judy and the baby could come home, but it seemed like weeks to me. I was so anxious to see the baby girl that Dad and Judy named Catherine Lynn. I didn't sleep a wink the night before the baby was to come home. I kept thinking how nice it would be to have a little sister to look after, and kept praying that Judy would be nice to her.

I waited in the car when Daddy went to pick up Judy and the baby, but I was busting with excitement. It seemed to take forever, but when I saw the nurses wheeling Judy out, holding my baby sister, I jumped out of the car and ran to meet them.

Judy complained of being tired, and went straight to bed when we got home. Daddy fixed dinner and took a plate of food into Judy. When Daddy asked her if she wanted to hold the baby, Judy let out with an angry, "Definitely not. That baby nearly split me in half, and I need time to heal. Just leave me alone!!"

The anger in her voice reminded me of the times at Nana's when Judy would go to her room and slam the door when she was mad or drunk. Daddy looked at me when he came out of their room, and slowly shook his head. "Your mother had an especially hard time having the baby, and she doesn't feel very well. We'll look after Cathy for a couple of days while your mother gets her strength back."

I was excited that Daddy had said "we" were going to look after the baby, but I wanted to tell Daddy that Judy wasn't sick, she was just hateful, but I held my tongue. Cathy was starting to fret, and after I watched Daddy change her diaper, he told me to sit in the big chair, which I immediately did. Then he picked Cathy up and we both burst out laughing as the diaper slipped down her tiny legs. "Guess I'd better try this again!"

Daddy said. I watched carefully as Daddy put the Diaper back on Cathy, trying to remember everything he did.

I sat back down in the big chair, and Daddy placed Cathy in my outstretched arms. He carefully explained about Cathy's neck resting on my arm so her little head didn't flop around. Daddy went to fix Cathy's bottle, and left me in heaven. I looked down into those big brown eyes, and swore I had never seen anything so perfect. Her little lips puckered up into a little pout, and at that moment this little creature stole my heart. I told her that I was her big sister, and I would protect her from all the bad things in this world—especially Judy.

Daddy said as soon as Judy was up to it, we would take a little visit to Nana's so she could meet Cathy. Judy agreed to the trip right away, probably because she knew Nana would take over the care of the baby.

When we pulled in front of Nana's house, I nearly broke my neck getting out of the car. I hadn't seen her in so long, and I couldn't wait for her to see Cathy. Nana was excited, too. She took Cathy in her arms and sat on the sofa as soon as we got in, and motioned for me to sit next to her. Judy had gone to lie down, expressing how exhausted she was. Daddy said he would run to the store, so Cathy, Nana and I were all alone.

"Isn't she beautiful, Nana?" I asked.

"She's a little angel. Can you believe you were ever this little?" I shook my head no at that.

"You know, while you're here, I'll show you the basics of taking care of a little one. That way you can help your mom and Daddy, and be a good big sister." When she said that, I knew she thought Judy wouldn't be a good mother. After all, she wasn't with me, so why would she change now?

Nana showed me how to feed Cathy, and showed me how to burp her, and how to put a diaper on that would stay. She would show me, and then the next time that something had to be done with the baby, she would let me do it—under her watchful eye and guidance. The time at Nana's went too fast, and it broke my heart to tell her goodbye. I didn't know how long it would be before I saw her, so I gave her a big hug and lots of kisses to hold us over.

Two days after we got back home; Daddy had to go back to work. Judy was still moping around the house, but at least she was out of bed. She would feed Cathy, and change her, but I never saw her hold Cathy just to cuddle or play with her, but I would sit in the big chair and hold her every chance I got.

Judy had just started feeding Cathy her bottle when Daddy left for work. He was no sooner out the door, when Judy told me to sit in the big chair. She placed Cathy in my arms, and handed me the bottle, and then went back to bed. I let Cathy drink from her bottle for awhile, but knew from watching Daddy and Nana that I would have to hold her over my shoulder and pat her back until she burped. I was trying to figure out how to get her to my shoulder and still support her little neck. I was terrified that I was going to do something wrong and hurt her, but I finally managed to do it, and was very proud of myself. After Cathy let out a big burp and spit up on my shoulder, I cradled her in my arms and fed her some more.

After a few weeks, I was very good at taking care of Cathy. Judy would pretend to be the doting mother whenever Daddy was around, but as soon as he was gone, she completely ignored her. I was happy to take care of Cathy. The further Judy stayed away from Cathy, the happier I was. At least I didn't have to worry about Judy being mean to her.

A few weeks after bringing Cathy home, Judy was ready to go out after Daddy left for work. She would always manage to be back before Daddy got home, but she would always be drunk. I was left to take care of Cathy and the house while she was gone, but Daddy had no idea what was going on. He thought Judy was drinking at home, and they would argue about it. Daddy would tell her, "You can't be a responsible mother if you're drunk all the time!" at which Judy would reply, "You try staying home all day with a crying baby! I just drink a little to help calm my nerves!" I hated to think how bad the argument would be if Daddy knew I was left alone everyday with Cathy. I didn't dare tell him for two reasons: I wouldn't want to see the pain in his eyes, and I definitely didn't want to endure the pain Judy would inflict on me if I told!

Cathy grew like a little weed. She was roly-poly and a happy baby. She would coo and giggle, and I loved her more with each passing day. I grew more confident with my mothering skills as time went by. I wasn't confident enough to give her a bath, although I had watched Daddy do it a couple of times. I didn't feel comfortable standing on a stool at the kitchen sink and trying to hold on to a slippery baby. When Daddy would give Cathy a bath, she would kick her feet and splash with her arms and giggle up a storm. I loved to watch her take her bath, but was wise enough to not try to give her one.

Cathy was 9 months old when I started school. I was excited about going, but worried about Cathy being left alone with Judy. I worried about Judy being mean to her, or just ignoring her altogether, or even leaving her alone while she went out, or even worse—taking her with her. The hours spent at school seemed endless, and I would rush home and change Cathy's soaked diaper, and fix her something to eat. She would eat like she was starving, so I knew Judy had been busy with other things—like drinking. But my fears of Judy leaving home were relieved when Daddy announced that he would be coming home for lunch. Since his lunch times varied, Judy would have to stay home or get caught.

Judy missed the milestones in Cathy's growing. I would talk to Cathy constantly when I was with her. She was great company for me, and she would always babble back. I would say "Dada" to her all the time, and was so excited when she said it herself. Daddy was beside himself with pride when he heard her. I didn't bother trying to teach her "mama" because I didn't think Judy deserved the title. After all,

Judy was hardly involved in Cathy's life. I tried to teach her to say my name and the "bith" she responded with was good enough for me.

Before I knew it, Cathy was sitting up, and then trying to crawl. I couldn't help but laugh when she would get herself into the crawling position, and then rock back and forth, as if she was trying to get up enough speed to take off. Then one day she did get going and the look of amazement on her face as she did so was unforgettable.

Judy was very grouchy all the time and seemed to drink more and more. Daddy told me that a lot of women were like that after they had a baby. I think he was making excuses for her, but I could see the disappointment in his eyes when he would come home and find her passed out. I was amazed that he hadn't realized that she was like that all the time, but he always tried to find good in everything.

Cathy was taken to the base doctors for checkups on a regular basis, but when she was two and a half, the doctors told Daddy and Judy that she was anemic, and she probably wasn't getting enough iron in her food. They said to give her lots of eggs and liver. I could get her to eat the eggs, but she would spit the liver out that Daddy cooked. On one rare occasion, Judy was feeding Cathy the liver, and she sprayed it all over Judy when she spit it out. Judy slapped her hard across her little cheek, nearly knocking the highchair over in the process. Cathy cried like her heart was breaking, and she had a red welt on her cheek for almost an hour. I was half hoping it would still be there when Daddy got home just to see how Judy would lie her way out of it, but unfortunately it faded away before then.

Cathy was trying to walk when she was a little over a year old. She would hold onto furniture and take a few steps, but it was a slow process. When she would try to take a few steps on her own, she would fall, tripping over her own feet. Daddy said it was natural at first, but as a month and then another passed, and Cathy wasn't getting more than a couple of steps before she fell, Daddy got worried.

Cathy saw a special doctor at the base, who told Daddy that Cathy was both knock-kneed and pigeon-toed, and she was in fact tripping over her own feet. They had special shoes made for Cathy, and in a few weeks, she was not only walking, but trying to run.

It was about this time that Judy announced that she was pregnant again. Daddy was excited at the news, and so was I to an extent. I was afraid that I wouldn't be able to take care of the things that had to be done from the time I got home till the time Daddy got back from work, because after Daddy had lunch and went back to work, Judy did absolutely nothing. I was only eight years old, but felt the weight of the world on my shoulders.

On Cathy's third birthday, there was snow falling and it was bitter cold. Daddy came home from work with cupcakes and party hats, and said "We aren't going to let a little snow mess up our celebrating!"

After dinner, we sang "Happy Birthday" to Cathy, ate the cupcakes and ice cream, and then Daddy gave her two packages to open. One was a beautiful baby doll with clothes to change, and the other was a new snowsuit and boots. Daddy had me get Cathy in them, and then get bundled up myself. Daddy got his coat and gloves one, and we three went out into the twilight and had a snowball fight, and built a snowman.

When we went back inside, Daddy had us get our pajamas on, and then fixed us hot chocolate. We were sitting at the table with him when he said, "I have a surprise for you. In May, I'm going to be sent to Japan. You and your mother will be moving to Springdale, where my family lives. We'll stop and see your Nana, because the new baby will be here by then, and then we'll get a new house in Springdale, and Lizbeth, you'll go to a new school."

"Is Japan by Springdale?" I asked.

"No, Japan is across the ocean. It's another country all together, so I won't be able to see you for awhile. But, I'm anxious for you to meet my family. You have another Grandmother, and all kinds of aunts and uncles that you've never met. I'll miss you all, and won't get to know the new baby until I come back, but the time will pass quickly, or I'll make arrangements for you all to come there. How's that?"

"Why can't we just stay with Nana?" I asked.

"Nana doesn't have much room, and it's about time you met my side of the family."

I had nightmares that night. Daddy was my protection from Judy's wrath, and he would be leaving. We would be in a strange place, with a new baby, strange people and a new school. I had a feeling that this was not going to be a good thing.

The next few months were almost too much to bear. Cathy was full of energy, and would be into one thing after another. Judy was grouchier than I had ever seen her, and would scream at Cathy at the top of her lungs over the least little thing. Then Cathy's feelings would be hurt, and she would pucker up and cry like her little heart was breaking. I would find bruises on Cathy many times after coming home from school, and when I would ask Cathy how she got her boo-boo, all she would say was "mama.' She didn't have to say anymore. I knew the torment she was going through, because I had been there so many times myself.

I worried about Cathy while I was at school, and my grades began to suffer. I was falling asleep in school, because I wasn't sleeping well at night. I had considered telling Daddy that Judy was hurting Cathy, but I knew Cathy and I both would pay a dear price if I did. One day the angels must have been watching over us. I was home from school because of a bad cold, and Judy was having a really grumpy day. Nothing I did would please her, and Cathy's playing was getting on her nerves. Suddenly she went into a violent rage, grabbed Cathy up, and flung her across the room. The front door opened just as she flung Cathy, and Daddy walked in. I had run to Cathy, who was a little heap on the floor. I held her close as I looked at Daddy. I had never seen such a look of rage on his face. He crossed the room in a gigantic stride, took Judy by her arms, shacking her violently, yelling, "If you weren't pregnant, so help me God, I'd knock the shit out of you!!! What the hell's wrong with you?? She's just a baby, for Christ's sake!!"

Judy jerked out of his grip and yelled back at him, "You should have to put up with these sniveling brats all day. I can't take this bullshit anymore—and pretty soon they'll be three. I'm about to lose my fucking mind!" Then she started crying hysterically.

Daddy turned away from Judy, knelt by Cathy and picked her up. He checked her carefully, and then gave her a big hug and kiss, saying, "It's okay, sweetheart. Mommy's not herself. It's okay."

It was very tense in the house that night. Cathy steered clear of Judy, and I knew that she was learning the lessons I had learned, and it made me sad that this was happening. I was getting her ready for bed, and started telling her about the angels who would protect her, like Nana had told me. Then Daddy came in to tell us goodnight, and told us that he had hired someone to come and help Judy with things around the house while he was at work. "Having a baby is very stressful and Mrs. McMichael will help with taking care of you, Cathy, and the housework. That way your mother will get plenty of rest, and have a healthy baby. She'll start Monday morning.

Daddy's announcement eased my mind. At least I wouldn't have my thoughts consumed with worries of Cathy's safety. I think Daddy's worries were laid to rest, also. I know that he thought this dark side of Judy was something new. If only he knew the truth about her cruelty. Who knows what the new baby will have to endure, because Daddy will not be around to protect us—he'll be far away in someplace called Japan. All I could do was pray for a future miracle.

Mrs. McMichael proved to be a blessing. Cathy was always clean and happy when I got home from school, the house was spotless, and Judy was in a halfway tolerable mood. A delicious dinner was always in the making, and by the time Daddy came home, the dinner was ready, the table set, and Mrs. Michael was heading out the door to tend to he own family. I wish I could count how often I wished that either Mrs.

Michaels could be our mother, or she could show our mother how to be like her. My wish never came true, and at the end of the day, Judy was still her selfish, hateful self, and still with us.

Daddy had officially gotten his orders to go to Japan. He was scheduled to arrive there the 15th of May. The movers were scheduled to start packing our belongings sometime in April. Daddy told me to sit aside anything that Cathy and I might want to take in the car to play with, but to limit it to two or three of the most essential items, because the station wagon could hold only so much. Daddy said his family in Springdale was looking for a nice house near a good school to rent, so that we could be moved in before he left for Japan.

Judy went into labor late in the evening on March 28th. I was as excited as I was when Cathy was born, but I didn't get to go to the hospital with Daddy this time. I had to stay home and keep an eye on Cathy as she slept. Mrs. Michaels would look in on us ever so often. About three o'clock in the morning Daddy drug himself in. I was wide awake on the couch, and he sat down and pulled me on his lap, whispering, "You have a strong, healthy baby brother. His name is Clifton Junior, but we'll call him CJ for short. Daddy is very happy!!!"

Then Daddy hugged me tight, carried me into my room, and tucked me into bed, kissing Cathy lightly on her cheek. I was dying to share the news of our baby brother with Cathy, but I knew that if I woke her up, she would be up the rest of the night, and Daddy looked very tired. I decided to wait till morning, and let Daddy get some rest.

The following morning, Mrs. Michaels was over bright and early. Cathy and I awoke to the smell of blueberry muffins. Daddy was already up, drinking coffee, and describing his new son to Mrs. McMichael. I had already told Cathy that she had a baby brother, but she was more interested in finding her dolly's dress than my news of CJ's birth. Daddy spoke proudly of his new son, and said that as soon as the Post Exchange opened, we would go find an appropriate outfit for his son to wear home.

Sure enough, we were at the Base Exchange a couple of hours later. They had an outfit for a baby that looked like a ball player's uniform, and Daddy said that was the one he really liked. Daddy was a baseball fan, so I wasn't surprised when he picked that one. I was surprised, however, when he picked out a little baseball glove and bat. I giggled when he laid it on the counter, and Daddy grinned at me and said, "Just a little something to spark the idea of pro ball. I always wanted to play myself, but the next best thing is having a son signed up."

Laughingly I said, "Daddy, he's just a little baby. He can't even hold a rattle yet, let alone a bat."

"Just give him time!" Daddy said, winking at me.

The next day Cathy stayed with Mrs. McMichael, and I went to school. The hours passed like days, because I knew Daddy would be bringing Judy and CJ home from the hospital, and I was anxious to see my baby brother. I ran full speed from the bus stop, and was out of breath when I flung open the front door. Daddy was holding CJ when I ran in, looking like he'd hit the ball out of the park. I sat in the big chair, and Daddy placed the bundle of blue in my outstretched arms.

Cathy and I both had dark hair, but CJ's hair looked like strands of spun gold, and light wisps' of brows and lashes over his blue eyes. While Cathy and I had darker skin, his was very pale, and he had ears like Daddy's that I didn't think he would ever grow into. He was long and thin, all arms and legs, and I could tell he was going to look like Daddy. Cathy had the features of both Daddy and Nana, and they blended together to make a beautiful little girl. I looked exactly like Judy, and although to some she was a striking woman, her dark personality made her ugly to me.

In the next few weeks, CJ filled out. He was a happy baby, and Mrs. McMichael was always saying what a good disposition he had. We could tell Daddy was very proud of him, because he made over him so much. One day I asked him, "Daddy, do you like CJ more than Cathy?"

(I didn't ask about myself, because I was adopted, and one of the little girls at school had said parents always love their own children more than the adopted ones).

Daddy looked at me very seriously, and drew me in close to him, "I'm sorry if you think I love CJ more than you girls. A father loves his children equally. But a boy carries on the family name, and if anything ever happens to me in the future, it will be up to your brother to protect this family. He's my son, and I love him dearly, but I love Cathy and you just as much, because you're my daughters."

I gave Daddy a big hug and kiss. He didn't know how loved he made me feel with his words, even if I was adopted. I couldn't wait to go to school and tell that little girl how wrong she was.

CJ was a month old when Daddy said the movers would be coming, packing up our belongings and loading them into a big moving van and taking them to Springdale. He told me to pick out a few toys to take in the care, but not too many, because we would have to take clothes and the bassinette for CJ. We had a station wagon, but with all we had to take, it would be cramped.

We were going to stop by Nana's on the way, so I was very excited about the trip, although the thought of Daddy going far away left me with a knot in my stomach. Once again I felt this was a bad idea. I put a couple of Cathy's toys and a couple of books for me aside for the trip. Then I put aside the pictures Cathy and I had drawn for Nana, so that we could give them to her when we stopped by. I wished once again we could stay with Nana, or that Daddy didn't have to go away, but I kept my wishes to myself.

A few days later, the packers came and packed our things, and the next day the big moving van came. Daddy said his Mother and sister had found a nice house for us across the street from a very good school. Daddy had sent them money to rent the house for us. We loaded the station wagon, and we headed for Nana's house. I opened my "Nancy Drew" mystery and started to read. Cathy started playing with one of her dolls, but we were only about an hour into the trip when she grew bored and wanted me to stop reading and play with her. CJ was sleeping soundly in the bassinet, and after playing with Cathy awhile, she fell asleep too. I read a little more, and then watched the towns and country fly past the car windows.

Before long, we pulled up in front of Nana's. She must have been watching for us, because she was out her door before the car stopped. I ran to her as soon as I got the car door opened, but Cathy hung back. She didn't remember Nana from her first visit, but she approached slowly after she saw Nana hugging me. Nana exclaimed how much we had both grown, and what beautiful young ladies we were becoming. Then she put her hands on her hips and declared, "I want to meet my new Grandson!"

Nana made over CJ telling Daddy that the baby was the "spittin' image" of him. "I hope he has your disposition," she said to Daddy. "Lord knows we don't want him to have his mother's!" Judy frowned at the remark, but I think she knew it was the truth.

We spent the night at Nana's and when we said our goodbyes the next morning, I could see tears in Nana's eyes. When I gave her a kiss goodbye, I couldn't help feeling that would be the last time I would feel her arms around me or hear her say "I love you, Sweetheart." As we pulled away, leaving Nana waving goodbye, I told myself I was just feeling so sad because of all the changes taking place, making the future look dark to me.

It took another eight hours to get to Springdale. Daddy had stopped a couple of times for us to eat and go to the bathroom, but by the time we arrived on the outskirts of town, the baby was fussy and Cathy was cranky, and we were all tired. His whole family was expecting us, so when we pulled up in front of his mother's house, they were all there to greet us. I couldn't remember seeing so many people at one time outside of church. There were aunts, uncles and cousins everywhere and we were hugged and kissed by them all. Daddy made a point of introducing us to them all, but names escaped me and all I could remember was a sea of faces.

One person did remain on my mind, and that was Daddy's older sister—Aunt Bernice, not for any other reason than I got a bad feeling when I was close to her. Her hugs were strained, and I could feel the tension in her voice when she talked. Her voice was an icky-sweet nice that dripped with sarcasm and distain. She reminded me of the wicked stepmother in 'Cinderella.' With her sly questions about Judy and Nana, I knew she was up to no good. I could tell she didn't care for me or Judy, but she made over Cathy and CJ like they were royalty. My suspicions were confirmed when I overheard her tell her husband, "I don't know why my brother married that little whore and adopted her bastard kid. She must have tricked him somehow!" She blushed bright red, when I stepped out from the shadows, and I know she was wondering how much I had overheard.

We stayed there at the house with Daddy's mother and his sister Grace. Aunt Grace was what everyone called an 'old maid.' She was in her early 50's and worked in a garment factory. She didn't drive, so she walked a block Monday through Friday to catch the bus to work, and then she took one back home in the evening. She and Grandma Sweeney lived in a big old house that was probably 40 years old, but it was well maintained. It had an apartment upstairs, and the main living quarters downstairs. We all stayed in the apartment, which was completely furnished. Grandma Sweeney told Daddy, "I don't see why you rented a house. Your family could have just stayed upstairs, and you could have saved that rent money."

I knew the idea of us staying there did not sit well with Judy, because she sort of rolled her eyes at me when Grandma mentioned it, and then I heard her tell Daddy later that night in the upstairs apartment, "under no circumstances would I live in this house without you being here. I can tell they all hate me, and it would be pure hell living here!"

Daddy tried to convince Judy for the next three days that his family didn't hate her. All of Daddy's sisters were very nice, and I really liked all of his brothers. But, when it came to Aunt Bernice, I had to agree with Judy. That woman hated us, no doubt about it. She was real nice to us when Daddy was around, but if he was out of earshot, Aunt Bernice would say something hateful to Judy. Judy would say something hateful back, and Daddy would walk in just as she did, and Aunt Bernice would tear up and act all hurt and say to Daddy, "I was only trying to help!" and run out of the room. Then Daddy and Judy would end up arguing. I realized Judy was enduring the verbal abuse she had inflicted on me for so many years, and was now getting a taste of her own medicine. I almost felt sorry for her.......almost.

We went to look at the house that Daddy's family had rented for us, and I really liked it. It had three bedrooms and a big fenced in back yard, and it was right across the street from the school I would go to. It would only take me a minute to cross the street and be at school.

Daddy had arranged to have all the utilities turned on beforehand, so the day the van arrived with our belongings, we could go ahead and move in. Daddy helped us get the house in order, and every day one of his sisters would pop in, often bringing something good to snack on. Aunt Bernice came one time, and looked around like she was inspecting a bug under a microscope. Aunt Bernice made the mistake of saying something to Judy while Daddy was gone, and Judy grabbed her by her hair and dragged her to the front door, Aunt Bernice screaming and flinging her arms the whole way, with Judy yelling, "So help me, I'll kick your fuckin' ass, and I don't give a shit what the hell your brother says!!"

Cathy and I watched in total shock and amazement. I couldn't help thinking that life in Springdale could be pretty exciting while Daddy was away and maybe I wouldn't have to worry so much about us kids getting beat up if Judy kept taking her anger out on Aunt Bernice.

Daddy left about a week after the battle between Judy and Aunt

Bernice had taken place. I remember how upset Daddy was when he heard what had happened. I heard Daddy on the phone telling Aunt Bernice that Judy was his wife, and learn to deal with that fact, whether she liked Judy or not. On the same note, he told Judy that Aunt Bernice was his sister, and she would have to keep her temper in check when dealing with her. "Bernice is bossy by nature. You just let her have her say, and then do what you want to. I can't be thousands of miles away and worry about my wife and sister doing battle everyday!" Judy promised Daddy that she would try to tolerate Aunt Bernice, and I'm sure Aunt Bernice made the same promise concerning Judy.

It was only two days after Daddy left that those promises were broken. I came home from school to find Judy and Bernice arguing over CJ's care. He had a red bottom, and Aunt Bernice was telling Judy that if she was a better mother, he wouldn't have a sore bottom. Judy shot back, "This from a woman who didn't even raise her own daughter, but had her mother do it. What the hell would you know about it?"

Both Cathy and CJ were crying at the top of their lungs. No doubt they could feel the tension in the air. I was so upset with both Judy and Aunt Bernice that I finally screamed, "Just Shut up!!" and grabbed up CJ and Cathy and took them in the bedroom and slammed the door shut. Behind that closed door, I realized what I had done, and sat with the two little ones, expecting a beating any time. To my surprise, Aunt Bernice left, and Judy opened the door and actually apologized for their behavior. That was the first time Judy had apologized for anything, and I didn't trust her. I felt like her mood would change at any moment, and that beating was lurking around the corner.

Weeks passed without incident. Aunt Bernice stopped by once in awhile, and a couple of times she brought Grandma and Aunt Grace with her. Judy never took us to visit any of Daddy's relatives (a point made by Aunt Bernice) and since Grandma and Aunt Grace didn't drive, she brought them to us. Both women behaved themselves while

Grandma was there, probably because they knew she would not tolerate their bad behavior. Both Grandma and Aunt Grace were "Christian women" and behaved accordingly. Their visit was centered on us kids, and we received their full attention. Grandma asked Judy if she would mind if Cathy and I started going to Sunday school at their church. Grandma said she would arrange for our transportation. I was surprised when Judy agreed to let us go.

We attended Sunday school on three Sundays. After church we would go to either Aunt Faith's or Aunt Jane's house for dinner. Cathy and I would play with all our cousins, and really enjoyed our selves, and looked forward to the following Sunday. Judy never attended the functions, but I don't know if that was by choice or if she just wasn't invited. The only down side was Aunt Bernice. She wouldn't always attend Sunday school or Church, but she would be at the Sunday dinners. Aunt Bernice would always corner me and try to pump information out of me concerning Judy—where she went, who she talked to, etc. I was smart enough to know that Judy had the power to make my life more miserable than Aunt Bernice, so my standard answer was an "I don't know" or just a shrug of my shoulders.

Aunt Bernice would have loved to know that Judy was going out in the evenings, and a couple of times she had stayed out until the wee hours of the morning, barely getting home in time for me to go to school. She talked all the time on the telephone to someone named Jack, and I suspect that's who she was spending her nights with. I had never seen the man; he was only headlights in the night. Daddy left for Japan on the 11th of May and Judy started talking to Jack on the 18th. I knew Judy was up to her old tricks, and I was thankful for Cathy and CJ, because I had to stay with them, rather than going with her and putting up with her disgusting friends.

The Friday before the Memorial Day weekend, the principal of my school came to my classroom to take me out of class. She said my mother was in the office, and I was going to leave school early because of a "family emergency." My body was gripped with fear—had something happened to Cathy Linn or CJ? Was Daddy and Nana alright? All sorts of horrible thoughts went through my mind.

Judy didn't look upset at all, which I was expecting if anything had happened to one of the kids or Daddy. She gave me more of a grimace than a smile and a wink, then turned to the principal and said, "Thank you so much, Mrs. Carpenter. I certainly appreciate you letting her leave early," grabbed my hand and practically dragged me out of the school, and didn't let up until we had crossed the street and were standing in our yard.

I didn't have a chance to ask Judy what was going on, but as soon as we got to the house—I really didn't want to know, because I knew it couldn't be anything good. There was a strange car sitting in front of our house, and an even stranger man sitting on the front porch. Cathy Linn and CJ were also on the porch. Cathy Linn was scrunched in a corner, looking scared to death. CJ was lying on a blanket on the floor, screaming as loud as he could. He was soaked to the bone, or hadn't been fed for quite awhile. Probably both were true, because I didn't know just how long the "strange" man had been there. The fact that he was there at all let me know that us kids were the last thing on Judy's mind.

I pulled away from Judy's grip, and glared at the stranger. He turned his frustrated look from Cathy to me. They ran up and down my body, and made my body feel like the palm of your hand after someone has spit it. Before I could say anything, Judy scampered over to the stranger and sat next to him, acting like a shy school girl. Using her 'this is a big fat lie' voice, her words were dripping with lollipops and honey as she said, "This is my friend Jack. He's going to take us for a ride to see where he grew up."

I reached down to pickup CJ, who had cried himself to sleep from sheer exhaustion. Something deep in my stomach told me this was not good, and it told me so loudly that I experienced a cramp. I tried to change the plan by asking Judy, "You can just leave us kids here. I can take care of everything, and you can have fun!" Trying so hard to sound enthusiastic, I looked Judy square in the eye and gave her a big smile.

"But I wouldn't want to go without my babies," she said in the same voice. I knew then that nothing good was going to come of this—she never wanted us kids around. "We'll pack the cooler and have a picnic and everything."

With that, Judy got up, took the baby from me, and motioned me in the house. I took Cathy by the hand, and we reluctantly followed her. Cathy looked up at me, her round eyes were dark pools reflecting fear and confusion. I squeezed her little hand confidently, and gave her a little wink and smile—my way of letting her know that everything would be alright. She understood, and gave me a weak little grin back. I felt guilty—here I was reassuring her that everything would be fine, yet I had this ache in the pit of my stomach that told me it wouldn't. I felt like I was lying to Cathy.

Judy had gotten the cooler out, and was standing in front of the Frigidaire with the door wide open. She was tossing things to 'Jack' and he was putting them in the cooler. "Here's that fried chicken from last night. How come nobody ate any?" she was saying to no one in particular. I was tempted to remind her that the night before she got drunk while she was frying the chicken, and then went on a drunken screaming performance when it was time to eat. I kept the little ones in the other room until Judy passed out. Then I fed them both, and got them in bed. Cathy ate a couple of bites off a chicken leg, so I finished it, but I was too angry to eat anything else. Cathy also ate a little of the mashed potatoes, but I still ended up putting a whole bowl full in the fridge.

Judy had handed Jack not only the fried chicken, but the bowl of mashed potatoes as well. I began to think that she was drunk again, or had been taking too much of her 'medicine.' I had never heard of anyone taking mashed potatoes on a picnic, but then again, I was only

8 and was a long way from knowing everything a person should. Jack put bottles of beer in the cooler. He also put in 2 quarts of milk, the glass bottles clinking loudly as Jack put them in the cooler.

Slamming the refrigerator door shut, Judy grabbed a cardboard box that was near her feet, and put in a loaf of bread, 3 Twinkies, a jar of pickles that Aunt Grace had given us, and a baby bottle, 5 or 6 diapers, and a roll of Scot towels. "Take the cooler to your car, and I'll bring this box," she sid to Jack. Turning to me, she said, "You get the brats."

Cathy Linn wanted her cuddle toy, and I grabbed up a couple of extra blankets for CJ before picking him up. I handed the blankets to Cathy Linn, and grabbed a quilt on our way out. I almost dropped CJ, but managed to get control, and held the quilt under him, cradling him on top. I was thinking—what are we going to sit on at this picnic? I didn't like sitting on the grass-because I would always get a bad case of chiggers, so I grabbed the quilt.

Judy was impatiently standing next to Jack's car, all 4 doors standing open. "Come on! Come on!" she was yelling at me. I put CJ on the seat of the car, and then helped Cathy. She was sitting right behind Judy, CJ was in the middle, and I would sit behind Jack. Judy grabbed the door before I could close it. "Get in the damn car," Judy yelled at me. So I ran around the car, figuring Judy would close Cathy Linn's door.

I jumped in the car, slamming the door behind me. Jack started the car and started to move down street. All of a sudden, there was a loud yell, and l looked in time to see Cathy Linn's door fly open, and her disappear out the door. I screamed her name, and Jack slammed on his brakes so hard that CJ and I almost flew off the seat.

I don't know who jumped out of the car faster—Jack or me. We both ran around the back of the car. Jack's face was ghost white, and my insides were shaking so bad I could hardly stand it. I think we both were expecting to see something horrific, but when we saw her, Cathy

Linn was sitting back on her haunches, screaming to high heaven. She was a little scraped up, and Jack checked her over good before he let her run to me. She clung to me like she was trying to crawl right into my very soul. The poor thing was scared to death. I carried her back to the car, moved CJ over on the seat, put Cathy Linn in the middle of the seat, and went around to the other side and held CJ on my lap. Jack made sure the doors were shut tight and locked.

Where was Judy during all of this? She was still sitting in the car with the radio blasting and acting like she didn't have a care in the world. The ache in the pit of my stomach suddenly got worse as Jack started moving down the road.

We were on the road about an hour or more, when Judy let Jack know she had to pee. Jack pulled off to the side of the road, and everyone found a place to pee. Cathy and I were side by side at a spot where I could keep an eye on CJ, who was sleeping on the backseat of the car.

We were on the road for another 4 or 5 hours. It was just starting to get dark. The rocking of the moving car and the hum of the tire meeting the pavement had lulled the little ones into a deep asleep. I fought sleep as if I would surely die if I missed a single building, person, or sign we passed. Something told me it was important to watch where we were going. I ventured to break the silence by asking Judy where we were, and all she said was, "We're in the Ozark mountains."

It was almost dark when we passed through what could have been a small town. There were a few houses, a gas station, and a little country store sitting off the highway. We drove for another 10 minutes or so, when Frank made a left turn onto a dark, bumpy dirt road. Judy woke from her slumber long enough to ask frank where we were. "We're almost to the old homestead!" was his reply, as he turned off the main road onto an overgrown cow path.

What was once a dirt road was full of pot holes, and overrun with tall weeds. It obviously had not been travelled much in the past. It was but a few minutes when Jack brought the car to rest in the overgrown yard of a long ago abandoned, ram shackled old farmhouse. Cathy and CJ stirred a little when the car came to a stop, but fell right back to sleep. Jack produced a flashlight, and him and Judy started walking towards the old farmhouse. I was not in any big hurry to get out of the car, so I sat with the little ones and watched the light disappear into the darkness.

I tried to fall asleep, but kept hearing strange rustlings and animal sounds coming from the woods. I locked all the doors, and hunkered down, holding the little ones close. Fear made the minutes turn into hours, and when I saw the first flicker of the flashlight, I pulled the guilt over the little ones and myself, holding my breath and praying that the dancing light was followed with Jack and Judy, hidden among the shadows.

I was glad to see them. CJ had started to get fretful. I knew he had to be starving—he hadn't had anything but about 1 quarter of a bottle since we left, plus I was sure he was soaked. Judy and Jack made it to the car, and I asked Jack if he could get some milk and the bottle out of the cooler so I could feed CJ. Cathy started announcing her hunger, so he also brought out the container of chicken. I handed Cathy a leg, and she started eating like she hadn't had food for weeks. CJ was so hungry he did battle with the nipple on the bottle until he finally got the first few drops in his little belly. I was hungry, but figured I would wait until CJ was full, and dry.

Evening melted into a dark, cloudy night. Judy and Jack, after eating, had wondered off with the flashlight. They were exploring the woods, or the dilapidated out buildings. I didn't know where they were, but I was wishing they were there with us. I had to go pee so bad, but I would have to get out of the car to do it. It was so dark outside the car that I could barely make out the old farmhouse. Strange noises were coming from everywhere, and bushes were rustling. The only light was from a pale moon half hidden by clouds. Nature got the best of me, and I knew I had no choice but to unlock the car, get out, and pee. I opened the door slowly, and the squeak from the hinges filled the night like thunder, causing a bunch of chattering and rustling in the surrounding woods. I was standing between the car and the open door, which gave a little security. I was so scared; I didn't even get my panties down before I felt warm pee inching down my leg. I quickly squatted, peed, and jumped back in the car, locking the door quickly.

The sounds of the night kept me awake for quite awhile. I wondered where Judy and Jack were, but sleep was creeping up on me, and I finally gave in. I didn't wake until the sun was just starting to peep over the horizon, and CJ was letting me know he was wet and hungry. Maybe today we would have the picnic and then go back home. At least, that's what I was hoping.

It had been cramped trying to sleep in the backseat of the car with Cathy Linn and CJ. Cathy was sprawled out to the point she was taking up most of the seat, and what little space was left was taken up by CJ and the little barrier I had built around him, so I had crawled over the front seat sometime during the night. Judy and Jack had not been back to the car that I knew of.

CJ's crying woke me. I knew instinctively that he was wet and hungry. I got out and opened the back door, found a clean diaper, and changed CJ there on the seat. Cathy Linn was rubbing the sleep from her eyes, declaring she was hungry. I told her to watch CJ while I went to find Judy or Jack to open the trunk.

The sun was barely peeking over the horizon, dew was still heavy on the leaves, and the birds were just waking from their slumber. I stood beside the car for a few minutes. The air was fresh and clean, and I breathed deeply for a second. I surveyed my surroundings, and decided that the faded, graying mass of wood must have been a beautiful house in its time. It reminded me of the houses where Nana lives, and a fog of sadness enveloped me.

I missed Nana and desperately wished for her strong arms around me, and her loving voice guiding me. I looked through the glass at

Cathy, her little hand soothingly patting CJ's tiny tummy trying to quiet his silent sobs. Suddenly, a wave of anger and resentment overwhelmed me, and I clinched my fists and bit down on my lower lip. I silently screamed to the world, "If we were with Nana right now, we would be waking up from a warm bed. We'd be sitting at a table loaded with hot biscuits and thick country gravy. We'd be holding hands and saying morning grace."

"Where are you Nana?" I asked with mute words, but the only response was Judy screeching, "Jack, where the hell are the damn car keys? I gotta get a beer!"

Judy had appeared from nowhere and was leaning against the side of the car, her legs crossed at the ankles. I glared at her with extreme hatred, and prayed she would feel it to her very core. Her core must have been pretty thick; because she looked at me as intently as her red streaked eyes would let her and popped off, "what, you roll off the wrong side of the car seat?" Her hysterical laughter at her supposed joke bent her over, slapping her thigh aimlessly.

I don't think I ever hated her more. Every muscle in my body ached to pounce on her, pummel her with my fist and pull every strand of hair from her head. I wanted to see pain and fear in those laughing eyes, but I was a motionless statue. CJ's crying filled my head, and the anger grew more intense. I took a step towards Judy when a bright light blinded me, my body grew very hot, and I sunk into an abyss of darkness.

I didn't fully comprehend what had happened, but when I opened my eyes, I was sprawled in the dirt, Cathy Linn patting my face with her pudgy little hands and a look of terror in her eyes, whimpering "Lizbeth, Lizbeth. Wake up!"

I came out of a grey fog, looked around and wondered why I was laying on the ground. I had a terrible headache, and thought at first Judy had hit me, but she was still leaning against the car, lighting a cigarette. Jack had appeared from somewhere and was kneeling beside me, asking Judy, "What the hell happened?"

"Damned if I know. She just went all white and keeled over," she replied without any real concern. Jack helped me to my feet, and then opened the trunk. CJ was still crying, but no longer the loud wail like before. He was sobbing hopelessly, probably thinking he was never going to get anything to eat.

"How can we warm the milk?" I asked Jack. He just shrugged and mumbled, "I dunno. Guess he'll have to drink it cold."

I took the cold bottle of milk out of the cooler and filled the baby bottle, with Jack's help. I walked around to the back seat, putting the nipple of the bottle in CJ's mouth. He sucked furiously at first, but when the first of the cold milk hit his belly, his eyes got big and he sort of gasped. But, he was too hungry to stop, and started sucking again. I knew that he would probably end up with a tummy ache, but I tried to hold him on my shoulder more than usual, rubbing his back in small circular motions, hoping it would help.

"Well, let's get you kids settled inside!" Judy was almost joyful when she said it.

"Aren't we going to have the picnic?" I asked, thinking, "You have picnics outside."

"We'll have the picnic later. I want you kids inside while Jack and I run to the store." She picked up the bag that held the bread and napkins and the baby's diaper bag. "Bring that cooler in the house," she yelled to Jack, and he said, "Yes, boss—right away, boss!" giving me a wink and a grin as he said it.

I held CJ in my arms as I stumbled across the rocky driveway, Cathy clinging tightly to end of my dress. I looked around at the place. It had seen better days. I could tell that it had once been an impressive two story farmhouse, busy with a farming family. The white paint on the wooden house had long ago faded and peeled, beaten and burned by too many unattended winters and summers. I noticed a couple of the steps had broken, or disappeared all together. Jack took a leap onto the rotting porch, and reached his hand out to Judy. She took it, and she half jumped—he half pulled her up there with him. I handed CJ up to Jack, and he quickly passed him to Judy. Then I lifted Cathy Linn, her little arms outstretched. Jack grasped her pudgy little hands and swung her onto the porch, Cathy Linn letting out a squeal of delight as he did it. I refused Jack's outstretched hands, opting to belly shimmy my way onto the porch, lifting my leg to meet it when I had shimmed my way back far enough.

As treacherous as the porch was, I dreaded seeing the inside of the house. My expectations were way too high! The wood floor had rotted in several places in what looked like the dining room. I looked up to see bare sky—a gaping hole in the roof stared back at me. The dining room and 'parlor' occupied the front part of the house, while the second story was built over the kitchen and a bedroom. I guessed the other room was a bedroom, because there was a dirty, paper thin mattress lying on the filthy floor. Somehow I knew that was where Judy and Jack spent the night.

The rooms were dark and smelled of rotting wood and urine. Wallpaper was peeling off the walls, and plaster was steadily making its escape from the walls. Nearly all the windows were broken, but the over growth outside blocked any sunlight that would want to sneak in. In the kitchen was the top of a kitchen table lying on top of four milk crates where the legs should have been, which meant the table top hit me knee high. There was no refrigerator or stove, and the sink was rusted, along with the pump handle that had at one time brought water to the kitchen.

CJ had finished his bottle and fallen asleep in my arms. I had Cathy Linn get one of his blankets out of the diaper bag and spread it on the rotting mattress, only because I could find nowhere else to put him, and I knew Judy was too engrossed in her own needs to worry about us. I laid CJ down, and he fussed for a couple of minutes, but soon drifted back to sleep. I started looking around, and finally had to ask, "Where's the bathroom?"

Judy and Jack started to laugh, and Jack finally said, as he walked to the back door and started tugging on it, "Girlie, this is an old, old house. It doesn't have a bathroom but the little two-holed one out back!"

Jack no sooner got the words out of his mouth, than he gave a mighty tug on the door and it went flying open, throwing him half-way across the room, landing on his backside in all the dirt. Cathy Linn started to giggle, but as much as I wanted to, I didn't. I didn't know Jack very well, but I had seen a few of Judy's 'gentlemen' friends get really mad when you laughed at them, and it doesn't take too many knocks to the side of your head before you learn to always be on guard.

Jack started laughing along with Cathy Linn, but her cherub face, big brown eyes and twinkling giggle would set anyone to laughing, but being a long legged gangly ugly duckling, I didn't even smile, but just walked over to the door where Jack was pointing, and peered out. About 50 feet from the back of the house stood a little shack, with a leaning door, sitting back in the bushes and weeds. Another milk crate was sitting upside down, where steps had once been. I certainly didn't like the looks of it, but had to pee too bad to find another place to go. I climbed from the floor to the milk crate, and then gingerly stepped into the weeds, watching intently for snakes.

The door to the outhouse was sitting at a precarious angle, open far enough for me to squeeze through. It was a good thing, since I never would have been able to budge it, what with the high weeds in front of it. It was dark and musty inside. I peered down one of the holes. The stench of long ago use was now a lingering memory, but the darkness held unknown dangers. Knowing this, I quickly brushed cob-webs aside, climbed up and squatted over the hole, watching intently for movement before doing so. I never peed so fast in my life, imagin-ing movement in every dark corner as I relieved myself.

Of course, there was no toilet paper around, and I didn't care, jumping down and pulling up my panties, not even bothering to 'drip dry.' At this point niceties were the furthest from my mind—I just wanted out of the creepy outhouse. I was in such a rush to get out, I slammed against the rickety door so hard, it busted it off the hinges. I didn't care and didn't look back. I just ran back to the house, up the milk crate, and into the decaying kitchen.

Jack had placed the cooler on the floor by the makeshift table. Everything else had been placed on top. I quickly checked on CJ, who was sound asleep, and joined the others in time to hear Judy say, "We need ice and more beer. Jack and I will run down to that little store and get it. You kids will be alright in here till we get back."

Then the two of them went out the kitchen door and around the house. I heard the car start, and its whining escape down the cow path. Cathy Linn clung to my dress-tail, and looked at me with wide curious eyes. Did she share the uneasiness I felt? I shrugged the feeling off, and pulled Cathy Linn's favorite doll from one of the brown grocery bags, and smiled when she squealed in delight. I pulled out other toys and took them to the foul mattress where CJ was still sleeping. I put a finger to my lips, silently telling Cathy Linn to play quietly. She nodded with understanding, and then entered the land of make-believe with her dollies.

Minutes turned into hours. I had busied myself for the biggest part of the morning by playing with Cathy Linn and feeding and changing CJ. When morning bled into afternoon, I arranged the food and diapers and such. Somehow I knew Jack and Judy wouldn't be back anytime soon. That feeling was reinforced as the shadows of twilight overtook the sunlight. I took Cathy to the outhouse a couple of times, and took advantage of the trips myself. The outhouse wasn't as scary with Cathy, probably because I felt I had to put on a brave front for her. It had taken quite a bit of coaxing on the first trip. Cathy didn't want to go into the eerie outhouse, let alone sit over one of the holes. She was terrified she would fall in, and only my holding on to her tightly convinced her to go. When she was finished, she asked, "Me hold you?"

As total darkness surrounded us, I was thankful that Jack had left the flashlight. I gave CJ his bottle, then took the quilt and spread it over the rotting mattress so the three of us could lay on it. I had the flashlight on as I listened to the steady rhythm of the little ones breathing, frantically shining the light in the direction of any noise I heard.

I determined that we would be safer if the mattress was in a corner, the walls (such as they were) our fortress against intruders. So, I grabbed the mattress by a corner, and slowly got it situated in a corner. It had taken quite awhile to get it exactly where I wanted it, and the sweat dripping from my forehead told me it had been difficult. I lay back down, content in the knowledge that the two windowless walls would protect us, and stretched quietly on the quilt, prepared to get some much needed sleep. Dust plumes flew as I plopped my head down on the mattress, and after a little coughing and sputtering, I settled down to sleep, leaving the flashlight dimly illuminating the room.

I was just descending into the loving arms of slumber, when I heard a rustling noise in the wall next to Cathy Linn. I was wide awake. I cautiously moved my hand towards the flashlight, and sighed with relief as my fingers curled around the cold metal. I swiftly swung it towards the wall, revealing a large rat, his red, beady eyes glaring. I let out a scream, Cathy Linn and CJ both woke up screaming, and the rat went scurrying off to parts unknown. I tried to reassure Cathy as I jumped off the mattress, grabbing its corner, and pulling as hard and as fast as I could. I told Cathy Linn we were going to go for a ride, as I started moving the mattress. Cathy picked up CJ, and soothed him back to sleep. I was amazed at my own strength. What had been a tremendous task a few minutes ago and had taken what seemed like hours had been accomplished in a matter of seconds.

I finally came to the realization that there was no 'safe' place in the room, and hoped that rat was as scared of me as I was of it. I slept fitfully, waking often to check on the little ones. It seemed like morning would never come. "They'll be back by morning," I silently prayed.

I saw the sun peeping over the horizon, heard the birds chirping, and away in the distance the faint bark of a dog. I turned off the flashlight, and got up to look around. Everything looked as it should, but I realized my prayer had gone unnoticed—there was no sign of the car, or Jack and Judy. Cathy put her arm around my leg, hugging it tightly. I didn't want to show my fear, so I pretended like nothing was wrong. "How about—we get CJ fed and changed—and we go exploring?"

Cathy Linn clapped her hands in excitement, unaware that I was terrified to venture out of the house. If Judy was on one of her drunken binges, no telling how many hours she'd be gone. I needed to get familiar with our surroundings, and that was the only reason I even considered leaving the house. I fed and changed CJ, making a mental note that there wasn't much milk left, and very few clean diapers. I climbed out the back door first. Cathy handed CJ down to me. I was a nervous wreck thinking we would drop CJ in the transfer, but everything went pretty good. I helped Cathy climb down to the milk crate, her little legs getting scraped in the process. She let me know about it, too. She chastised me for the first 10 minutes of our 'exploration.' Then spent a few more minutes whimpering sadly about the boo-boo I caused her to get.

I had picked up a small board that had been laying against the house, probably a discarded part of it. I told Cathy to stay behind me, and to stay close. I knew she would when she grabbed my dress and clung tightly. I held CJ as high as I could with one arm, swinging the stick through the tall grass with the other. I started singing 'Jesus Loves Me' and Cathy Linn joined in. I was hoping that the commotion would scare away any 'varmints' lurking nearby, a trick Gramps had taught me.

I would stop every view minutes to get my bearings, and to rest a little. CJ was just a little baby, but with each step he seemed to get heavier and heavier. I have no idea how long it took to reach what had once been a path. It was overgrown, but they weren't nearly as tall as the weeds we had encountered before. There were patches of dirt in between the weeds, and I picked one and plopped down. Cathy Linn plopped down next to me.

I started thinking. The house was behind me. There's an old barn in front of me, and a gate to my right. Judging from what paint was left on it, I'd say the barn had once been red. It must have stood tall and proud in its prime, but the ravages of time had taken its toll. There had been lean-tos on both sides of the structure, but they had long-ago collapsed inward, clutching its weakened walls in desperation.

The path ran from the road between the house and barn and stopped at a half-open, wobbly wooden gate. I was trying to decide if the barn would be our quest for the day—or would we head towards the gate. After three eanie-meanie-minies, the barn won, a fact I was not too happy about. The barn would be dark; there would be cob-webs and maybe bats. I have no idea what made me think of bats, but the sheer thought of the sinister little pests gave me a chill.

"Let's see what's on the other side of the gate," I said eagerly to Cathy Linn. We both got up reluctantly, and I felt a pang of guilt as I picked CJ up out of the dirt. I knew I shouldn't have put him there, but my arms were so tired. "Laying him in the dirt was the only way my arms could rest," I said unconvincingly to myself.

CJ gurgled and cooed when I picked him up, not caring where we were going, just along for the ride. We managed to get to the gate in about 10 minutes. We rested there for a few minutes and then trav-elled on. The gate wouldn't budge when I tried to push it open further. It was open just enough for Cathy to squeeze through. I handed CJ to Cathy while I climbed over the gate, getting scratched by a rusty nail or wire, throwing my stick over before me. I picked up the stick, took CJ, and we started on, Cathy hanging firmly to my dress.

I headed for a wooded area off to my left. It sat about a hundred yards adjacent to the barn, but further back. It didn't take us too long to reach a small clearing under a big oak tree. It overlooked a grassy pond bank, and I could tell it had been the scene of many picnics. The pond was full, probably spring fed, but a slimy green moss floated on top of the water. I put CJ under the tree on a soft blanket of grass. He was starting to get fussy. He needed to be changed and was probably hungry. I hadn't planned for our outing to take so long, and hadn't brought a bottle or diaper.

"You keep close watch on CJ. I'm going to run back to the house to get a bottle and diaper," I said to Cathy Linn.

"Bring me some chicken," she answered back.

"Why not," I thought to myself. We were suppose to have a picnic, and what better spot. I ran back to the house, following the temporary path we had forged through the weeds. I was more careful climbing the gate, and was back at the house in no time. I quickly fixed the bottle, not worrying about the temperature, since it had been sitting out so long. I grabbed a diaper, a rag, one of CJ's blankets and wrapped two pieces of chicken in a napkin, threw it all in one of the paper grocery sacks, and headed back to the tree. I carried the stick in one hand, and the paper sack in the other. I figured the trail had been traveled enough to scare any snakes, but I held on to the stick-just in case.

I made it to the gate in no time, and scooted the bag through the opening, threw the stick over, and climbed over myself. I could hear CJ's wails in the distance, and knew he was demanding food. I raced to the clearing and found Cathy trying to hang on to CJ, who was flailing his arms and legs angrily. "I sang to him and everything-but he won't stop crying," she said, big tears welling in her eyes.

"That's cause he's hungry and wet," I said to Cathy. "You did good," I said reassuringly, patting her on her back.

I took CJ from Cathy, but I didn't know which end to take care of first. I decided he would be more comfortable drinking his bottle if his bottom was dry, so I laid him on the grass and took off his diaper. He was messy—and I was thankful I had thrown a rag into the bag. I crept down to the edge of the pond, tried to move the green moss out of the way, and plunged the rag into the water. It was cold, and I felt sorry for CJ as I rung the rag out. I started to clean his bottom with the cold rag, and he drew a sharp breath in, held it for a minute, and then let out a sorrowful howl.

I cleaned the tiny but as best I could, noticing that it was getting awfully red looking. I put his clean diaper on him, and gave him his bottle, which he attacked furiously. He sucked on the bottle fast and hard at the beginning, but then let up after awhile. He gave a couple of good burps and the drifted off to sleep. While I was feeding CJ, I told Cathy about the chicken, which she devoured instantly. She eyed the second piece so longingly that I finally told her to go ahead and eat it.

I didn't know how long we'd been gone, but it was getting pretty late in the afternoon. I washed out the rag and dirty diaper as best I could, telling Cathy Linn we'd hang it to dry somewhere in the house when we got back. I picked up CJ, grabbed the rag and diaper, and handed the stick to Cathy Linn.

We started on the trip back to the house, Cathy swinging the stick to and fro—almost bashing her head in a couple of time. We were at the gate in a short amount of time, and Cathy Linn squeezed through it once again—with stick in tow. I passed CJ to her, and when I got on top of the gate, looked all around for a car -- or Judy –or Jack. Nothing had changed.

The days passed slowly, with no sign of anyone. At first, I was angry at Judy for leaving us for so long, just to have fun. By the fourth day, worrisome thoughts filled my head. What if Judy was dead? That thought did not bring sadness, but rather a more terrifying thought—if she was- no one knew where we were. What would we do?

I cried silently at night out of an overwhelming sense of fear and frustration. After the second night, I instinctively knew that Judy wasn't returning anytime soon, if ever. After my hushed bouts with tears, I would lie awake and make plans for the next day. I used the flashlight only when needed, because I had heard Judy cussing about having to change the batteries before we left. I didn't know how long batteries lasted, but I knew it wouldn't be forever.

I also knew the milk, which had already started to sour, would not last forever, either. We would need that for CJ. While exploring the barn one day, I found a dirty glass jar and was inexplicably excited. The next day, at the pond, I washed it out as best I could and filled it with murky water. With Cathy Linn's help, I was able to get her, CJ, our sack—and the water back to the house.

We spent as much time as possible by the pond. It was springtime, and the field was fresh with the new buds of spring. The sun would shine, and Cathy Linn would bring a toy to play with, and I would enjoy the clean air and watch CJ sleep while butterflies flitted under the branches of the big tree.

I tried to keep us as clean as possible. I would wet a rag everyday and wash all our faces and hands, facing much resistance from Cathy Linn and CJ. I wasn't too happy about it myself. The water was cold, and no matter how much I rinsed it out, it still had a sour odor.

We had only brought 6 diapers for CJ, so I tried to keep them rinsed out and pray that one of them would be clean when one was needed, which proved impossible. I finally would only change diapers when he pooped and his once pink little butt soon became an angry fire-red. He screamed in agony every time I changed him. I would hold him close and rock. I felt so bad; I would start to cry myself. "I'm sorry CJ. I just don't know what to do," I exclaimed.

The fifth day there was a terrible storm. The wind roared, and thunder rumbled with lightning flashes striking all around the old house. I was sure the wind was going to blow it to bits, or crash it in on top of us. We huddled close on the mattress under the quilt, watching the rain pour in the other room through the hole in the roof. The storm ended by morning, and eased into a slow, steady rain.

We had been spending so much time at the pond, the house had gone unexplored. I made a game of it with Cathy Linn. We found an old pot in one of the abandoned cabinets, and a rusty fork and spoon in one of the drawers. Cathy Linn spent some time marching around the room, banging the bottom of the pot with the spoon—making 'moosic.' I clapped in time to her banging, and even followed her around a couple of times.

There were large chunks of white floating in clear liquid in the milk bottle, and there were only a few slices of bread remaining. I poured what little rain had collected in the pot into the jar, and then crumbled a slice of bread into it. After the bread absorbed the water, it was only half full. I poured some of the liquid and chunks from the milk bottle, and stirred and chopped with the spoon. I put some of this in the bottle to fed CJ.

He was hungry. He sucked as hard as he could, but couldn't seem to get any to come out. He kicked and flailed in frustration. I laid him on the mattress, and took the top off the bottled. There was a white mass stuck in the nipple—too big to go through the hole. I looked around helplessly. I had seen Nana make the hole bigger in a nipple with a knife, but I wasn't afforded such a luxury. I took a small bit of the rubber between my teeth, and ripped a piece of it out. The hole was a little bigger than I desired, but the deed was already done. I resumed feeding CJ, trying to adjust the bottle so he wouldn't choke.

Cathy and I shared the remaining concoction, both of us scrunching our noses at the rank flavor, but we ate as much as we could stand. We played hide and seek, and other childish games, until darkness lurched about and stole the day, thrusting us into the uncertainties of night.

By the tenth day, CJ's little body was so frail, you could count his bones through his pale, parchment like skin. He no longer cried, but whimpered with the soft mew of an orphaned kitten. He rarely opened his eyes, and his poops (what few he had) were nothing but liquid. His bottom was a slab of raw meat—so tender that he flinched if I so much as touched it. The air on his bare bottom seemed to afford him a small bit of relief, so often I laid him on his belly, hoping the clean air and warm sunlight would heal his blistered flesh.

Our activity waned with each passing day, content to sprawl listlessly on the tattered, dirty mattress or lay beneath the tree at the pond. Our lips were cracked and swollen. Cathy Linn's hair was matted and tangled, an occasional leaf or stem popping through the dark strands. Her little pink dress was now torn and tattered, and so dirty the pale pink barely shone through. Her skin was covered with oozing sores, and her eyes looked lost and empty when she looked up at me. CJ barely ever whimpered any more. I actually had to wake him up to eat, and he never let a sound louder than a whisper.

I knew I was in the same shape as them, and I also knew that Judy or Jack was never coming back. I had only a few crumbs of bread to crumble in the murky water from the pond. I had mixed the mashed potatoes in the water and milk until they were gone. The twinkies we had eaten the first night, and the chicken was all gone by the third day. The milk had long ago gone, and I strung out the ration of bread crumbs as long as I could, but tomorrow would see the last of any of the food we brought from home.

I sat watching the two little ones sleep, and tried to figure a plan for survival. I might be only eight, but my world of cartoons and fairy tales had long ago disappeared. I knew that people have to eat to live, and if they don't-they die. I wept in frustration, knowing that I had to do something while I was still able, my sobs falling quietly on the silence around me.

That shroud of silence was broken by a distant honk of an automobile—long and faintly loud at first, then fading off into distance. I had forgotten all about the highway. Well, I hadn't really forgotten it—it just never crossed my mind because I had been waiting for someone to rescue us. It had been 16 days—no one was going to rescue us. We would have to find our own way back—and the highway would play an important role in our achievement of that.

I snickered at myself for using the terms 'us' and 'we.' I was a backwoods eight year old, with a three year old toddler, and an infant who barely held the dark angel of death at bay. I knew we had to leave what meager security the house offered and travel towards the road. Could we do it? Who knew how far away that blacktop was? And then, who knew how long before help came?

I didn't have any of the answers, but I knew one thing. Getting to the blacktop was the only thing to do. We might make it, we might not. But, at least there's a 'might' involved. We had stayed put for 16 days-and nobody came. If we stay another 16 days—nobody will come; there's no 'might' involved.

I tickled Cathy Linn awake. I wanted her in an agreeable frame of mind, because she has a stubborn streak in her that will not go away. I knew I had to be enthusiastic and make everything a game if I wanted to maintain her interest and cooperation.

I used my 'fairy princess' voice as she awoke to the tickling. "Guess what, Cathy Linn?" I asked with a mysterious flair. "The head fairy said we have to make a trip to their village, so you can be crowned Princess."

"I don't want to make a trip," she said with a pout, adding, "I'm hungry."

"If you could have anything in the world to eat right now, Cathy Linn, what would it be?"

She put her finger up to her chin and thought pensively. "Annnything?" she asked, drawing the word out in disbelief?

"Yes, anything," I answered. She jumped up, and started bouncing around—a burst of energy that didn't have a very long duration. "Twinkies!!" she exclaimed. My mouth watered at its mere mention. I patted the spot next to me on the mattress, held her cherub cheeks in my hands and with the sternest voice I could muster I said, "When we get to the village, you can have all the Twinkies you want. But, it's going to be hard for us to get there, because the evil fairy doesn't want you to be Princess. I will guard you and get you there—but you have to give me a pinkie-swear that you will do what I say on the trip—even if you get mad or tired."

Her big brown eyes were round with excitement and expectation, with a little fear mixed in. "The evil fairy doesn't want me to be Princess?" she asked, puzzlement in her voice. "Why doesn't she like me?"

"I don't know—she's just evil. We'll fool her, though!" We entwined our pinkies and Cathy Linn swore she would listen to me on our adventure. I retraced our trip that brought us here over and over in my mind. I knew we had passed a store and it had only seemed like a few minutes after that we turned left onto the wooded path that was trying to pass as a road. But, we were in a car. What only took minutes to accomplish in a car might take us days on foot—but we had no choice but to give it a try. I took what water we had from the pot, poured part of it in CJ's bottle and the rest in the jar. I ripped the tattered remains of a curtain from one of the windows, tore it in strips and tied it around the jar, with another piece serving as a handle. "You'll have to help carry the water. I'll carry CJ and the flashlight," I told Cathy Linn.

I took the quilt from the mattress, and folded it in a triangle. I tied a sturdy knot with the two corners, and then placed it over my head and across one of my shoulders. After forcing CJ to drink some water from his bottle I tucked him in the little pocket of the quilt, along with his blanket and the diapers, laying the flashlight at his feet, and picked up my stick. It was mid-morning. The sky was clear and bright, and I looked at Cathy Linn and said, "It's time to go."

The trek went pretty good at first. Cathy tried to skip at first but I hollered, "Cathy Linn—you'll spill all the water!" She came to an immediate stop, pursed her lips together and mumbled, "Sorry."

"It's okay. You didn't know better," I replied. We moved at a pretty good pace for the first hour, but then we both grew tired, and our steps got slower and slower until we just stopped. I didn't know how far we'd travelled, but Cathy and I were exhausted. We found a little clearing on the edge of the woods, and rested for a while. I gave CJ some water, and then the two of us took a drink and started off again.

We would walk for a few moments, then rest a few moments. Cathy kept asking, "Are we there, yet?" I would lose my patience and yell at her, then she would pucker up and cry—and I'd feel bad. Then we'd make up and everything would be fine for awhile. CJ, on the other hand, hardly even moved. He never cried, or even whimpered, anymore. When we stopped, I would force the nipple in his mouth, and he would instinctively give a couple of feeble sucks. I didn't know if he was getting water or not, but prayed he was getting a few drops.

Things weren't going the way I had hoped. In my mind we would be at the little store, hoping the clerk would give us a Twinkie and help us find Judy-or someone by mid-afternoon. However, twilight was enfolding us, and I realized we would be spending the night in the woods. I searched for a place that would shield us from the evils of night, and was thrilled when I spotted a rotted out tree trunk. I placed CJ on a bed of leaves, and shined the flashlights beam into the dark opening. I took the stick and scraped it around the floor of the cavity, ready to jump out of the way if a snake reared its ugly head. No eyes shined in the light, and there was no movement of any creatures. The little cubbyhole was perfect for the three of us.

Darkness had completely surrounded us by the time we got settled in. I spread one of CJ's blanket on the dirt. Cathy Linn crawled in first. I handed CJ to her, and then I crawled in. I lay facing the opening, trying to see in the darkness that was black as ink. I held the stick close, and after shedding some silent, angry tears, fell asleep.

Morning came softly, and I slowly opened my eyes to a beautiful spring day. Right outside the opening, a doe was casually nibbling grass. Every once in awhile her head would pop up, and she would carefully survey the surroundings. I wanted so much for Cathy Linn to see her striking beauty, but knew if I uttered a sound or moved an inch—she would be gone. So I watched her graceful movements until she was out of sight. Maybe she was a sign from God that today would be wonderful! I tried to keep that optimistic outlook as we prepared to continue our journey.

We moved at a snail's pace, reaching the blacktop road early afternoon. We did a little dance on the hot asphalt but were disappointed that no one was around to help celebrate our arrival. I knew we had turned left to get to the house, so we would go to the right to get to the little store. A couple of cars passed us on the road, but none stopped to give us a ride. In their defense, I didn't try to flag them down. I wanted to, but I didn't trust anyone enough to ask for help. They probably thought we were local kids on an outing.

We topped a hill and in the little valley below sat the little store. It was a little one floor building made of rock and mortar, stretching low and lean over its little spot on the road. There were two gas pumps out front, and a crooked porch roof protecting the door. Two old farmers sat in cane chairs on the porch, surveying and no doubt passing commentary on those passing through the store's portals.

I'm sure they watched our slow approach to the store, probably trying to figure out whose 'youngins' we were. They looked a little shocked and puzzled as we climbed the solitary step to the porch. We were ragged and dirty, matted hair and torn clothes. I'm sure we looked as if we'd been spit from the bowels of hell. They said nothing, but slowly got up from their chairs and followed us inside, eager to hear the facts so they could spread them diligently.

The door opened onto a large but cozy room. Makeshift shelves filled most of the room. To my left was a wood table with 4 or 5 chairs scattered around it. Three of the chairs were occupied by grizzly old men, clutching a cup of steaming coffee, their jaws dropping upon our entrance. A portly woman stood among the men, holding a large black coffeepot. Her gray bun sat demurely at the nape of her neck, and her supple, round curves and soft green eyes reminded me of Nana.

My heart ached for Nana. My mind screamed in anger and frustration and pain for me and my siblings. Why would our mother leave us?

Did she hate us that much, or was there a logical explanation—like an accident? The emotions overwhelmed me. I stood there like a doe caught in headlights, clutching CJ and watching Cathy Linn devour one Twinkie after another.

The woman rushed to me, and I handed her CJ as soon as she reached me. She took one look at him and started shouting orders to the men. "Bubba, you go get Doc and tell him to come right now!! Frank, you call the Sheriff and tell him we got us a situation here that needs his immediate attention. Charley, you hang onto this baby while I tend to these little ladies."

She handed CJ to Charley and knelt in front of me, caressing my arms tenderly. "Who are you child? You don't belong to any folks around here—one of us woulda recognized ya? Who you belong to? Where you been? How did you get here? Where's your mama and daddy?"

"My name's Lizbeth, and that's Cathy Linn. CJ's my baby brother. Nobody. We were at a house up the road. We walked. I don't know." I answered her questions in the order she asked them, exerting as little energy as possible. My knees suddenly turned to jelly and a dark fog overtook me, and I crumbled into a helpless mound of flesh on the dirty store floor.

I could hear faint voices in the background as strong hands lifted me. I floated through the air and came to rest on a very rough, hard surface. I felt a cool rag being dragged softly across my face. I tried to open my eyes, but my mind wouldn't let me. I was floating on a cloud of nothingness—no pain, no fear, no responsibilities. I wanted to just linger there for awhile—just a little while.

Then a gruff voice broke through my cocoon of semi-consciousness. "I'd say we have quite a situation here, Wilma. You manage to get any info on these youngins'?"

I opened my eyes cautiously, peering around me. At my side sat Cathy Linn, gobbling down Twinkies and milk. A man had CJ on the hard, cold counter—but CJ entered no protest. He lay motionless. A man was holding a stethoscope to his thin, pale chest, shaking his head slowly.

"He's barely alive. We have to get him to the hospital right away," he exclaimed. "Sheriff, how fast can you make that car go?"

"As fast as need be," the sheriff shot back. "Doc, you climb in back with the baby. The girls need to go too. I think we have a lead on who they are. I'll have someone from Springdale meet us at the hospital."

Wilma helped me from the table and guided me out to the sheriff's car. Charley had carried Cathy Linn behind us, and placed her tenderly on my lap.

Wilma knelt by the open car door, caressing my arm gently, she leaned over and gave me a loving kiss on my cheek.

"Don't you worry child, you're safe now."

The door closed with a loud thud, and as we pulled away with lights flashing and sirens blaring, for some unexplained reason, I believed her.

CPSIA information can be obtained at www.ICGtesting.com
Printed in the USA
LVOW12s2229030714

392729LV00004B/6/P

9 781432 727567